Please Return
To

Robin Robinson

CHERRY AMES, DUDE RANCH NURSE

The CHERRY AMES *Stories*

☆   ☆   ☆

The VICKI BARR *Flight Stewardess Series*

"I have never mentioned the check to anyone!" Mrs. Blair shouted.

CHERRY AMES
DUDE RANCH
NURSE

By

JULIE TATHAM

~~~~~~

NEW YORK

GROSSET & DUNLAP

Publishers

Contents

CONTENTS

CHERRY AMES, DUDE RANCH NURSE

CHAPTER I

Tucson, Arizona

"WELCOME TO THE SUNSHINE CITY!" CHERRY STARED forlornly at the big placard. Tucson certainly deserved its nickname, but there was nobody at the Municipal Airport to welcome *her*. The waiting room, a glass-fronted portion of three huge hangars, made her feel as though she were surrounded by miles and miles of planes. After a while she wandered over to a bench and sat down with her suitcase and coat at her feet.

What could have happened to Kirk?

When Cherry had left her home in Hilton, Illinois, it had been snowing hard. And when she boarded the plane in Chicago that morning, she had been grateful for the warmth of her interlined coat. But now, here in Arizona, although it was five o'clock on a Sunday after-

1

noon in late February, she was almost too warm in her smart red flannel suit and wished she had worn her white Nylon blouse instead of a sweater.

But she had been told that as soon as the sun dropped down behind the mountains the air would grow steadily cooler and so she had packed in her bag some twin sweater sets and a warm sports jacket. In the bag, too, were seven white uniforms and caps, a bathing suit, T-shirts, a bright checkered cowboy shirt which her twin brother, Charlie, had given her, blue jeans, donated by her father who said that in Arizona they were called "Levis"; new, shiny riding boots, a gift from her mother, and from Cherry's harum-scarum young neighbor, Midge Fortune, an atomizer containing Cherry's favorite brand of perfume.

Midge, Cherry knew, had worked hard to earn the money for that perfume and atomizer, and so she hadn't had the heart to tell her that perfume—in fact, any kind of cosmetic—was taboo at the Hacienda de dos Montes —the Twin Mounds Guest Ranch. At least so far as the resident nurse was concerned, because several of the guests were asthma sufferers. Some asthmatics were allergic to perfume; even a faint whiff could have as disastrous an effect upon their breathing as pollen-laden air had on hay-fever sufferers.

Cherry had received this new assignment through an old friend, young Dr. Kirk Monroe, who had been her boss on the *Julita* when she had been ship's nurse during a cruise to the Caribbean. Two weeks ago, while she was working in the Hilton Clinic, Cherry had received a letter from Kirk.

"Dear Cherry," he had written. "As you know, I resigned as the *Julita's* ship's surgeon in order to specialize in Pediatrics. But before I could take advantage of the residency that big New York City hospital offered me, my folks out here asked me to come back home. There's a great shortage of M.D.'s in Tucson (pronounced Toosahn, in case you don't know!), especially during the season when so many people who suffer from asthma, rheumatism, arthritis, and such, visit our 'Sunshine City.'

"There is also a dearth of R.N.'s from October to May, and that's one reason why I'm writing you. Very good friends of mine, Frank and 'Señora' Conrad, own a guest ranch about forty miles from town. Ten of the guests, all of whom are asthmatics, live in the house proper. The others, forty-or-so at the moment, occupy the cabins. They're perfectly well. The asthmatics, five of whom are teen-agers, are my patients. Señora herself is an R.N., but she is too busy most of the time helping Frank run the hacienda to do much nursing. Not that there's much nursing to do, but you can see that the Conrads have to have a resident nurse throughout the season. Recently they've been having trouble. The nurses come and go. The old battle-ax who's the present incumbent has given two weeks' notice. The trouble is, I think, basically a personality problem.

"But you, Cherry, have the uncanny knack of being able to get along with everyone, and are especially good with kids. I think you'll like the job and have a lot of fun. And you'll go back home the end of May full of Vim, Vigor, and Vitality. Think of it as a vacation. Outside of just being there in case one of my patients has an attack, and charting the T.P.R.'s in the A.M. and P.M., your time will be pretty much your own.

"There is, however, one hitch which I don't think will bother you at all. The resident nurse is supposed to assist the resident tutor in the supervision of the teen-agers. This means eating at the same table with the kids; making sure that they rest for an hour after lunch and for an hour after dinner and that they obey the Lights-Out-at-ten-o'clock rule.

"Part owner of the ranch is a handsome young fore-man, named Torrington, who will be delighted to give you riding lessons if you're a novice. There's an enor-mous swimming pool, too, and it's not off bounds as the one on the *Julita* was."

Kirk had ended the letter begging her to accept this new job. It had arrived on a week end when Charlie was home from college. Cherry's tall, blond twin had practically ordered her to accept, and her parents had heartily agreed with him that this was a "chance of a lifetime."

When Cherry had consulted Dr. Joe Fortune who had brought the twins into the world, he said:

"Go by all means, Cherry. You've been working too hard at the clinic. Three months of sunshine and that wonderful Arizona air are just what your old family doctor orders."

So Cherry had wired her acceptance, and at Charlie's advice had taken ten riding lessons at the Hilton Academy. Now here she was in the Tucson airport, but there was no sign of the handsome young doctor who had promised to meet her. Cherry remembered Kirk Monroe as being as tall and well-built as Charlie, with gray eyes and thick, wavy brown hair. He had been deeply tanned when she had last seen him shortly after the *Julita* docked in New York City, and was probably as brown as an Indian now.

Several tall, handsome, tanned men came into the waiting room, but none of them was the doctor. They all glanced at her not once, but twice, because Cherry, even without make-up, was that kind of person. She was tall and slim with short, crisply curling black hair and dark-brown eyes. Even now when she was tired and feeling rather forlorn, her cheeks, which had earned her her nickname, were the color of American Beauty roses.

Seated on the bench opposite Cherry was a prosperous-looking white-haired gentleman who had boarded the plane with her in Chicago. Cherry knew his name because the stewardess had called him Mr. Fleming when she gave him the little special attentions which very important passengers on air liners usually demand.

Mr. Fleming, like Cherry, was obviously waiting for someone who was late. He kept glancing at his expensive wrist watch, crossing and recrossing his legs impatiently. Cherry was so lonely that she was on the verge of saying to him "We were on the same plane and now we seem to be in the same boat," when suddenly a tall but not at all handsome young man came into the waiting room.

He towered head and shoulders above everyone else in the crowd and reminded Cherry of a giant puppet because he was so bony and moved with such jerky, clumsy strides. He looked worried, too, for his eyes blinked behind his huge horn-rimmed spectacles as he scanned the waiting room. He didn't even glance at her as he stopped with a stiff, awkward bow in front of the white-haired gentleman.

"Mr. Fleming?" he asked in a nasal voice.

"Right. Harold Bean?" The two men shook hands and Mr. Fleming said rather crossly, "What kept you? I told you on the phone yesterday that I would have to leave for the Coast on the midnight plane. You're not like your father who was always very prompt."

"Please accept my apologies, sir," Mr. Bean said pedantically. "We are, at the present time, quite under-staffed at the ranch. I had an extremely difficult time getting away."

Cherry tried not to listen, but the giant "Pinocchio" had such a penetrating voice that she would have had to cover her ears in order to avoid eavesdropping.

"Never mind, never mind," Mr. Fleming was saying impatiently. "Let's get along. I want to see that mine."

"Impossible," Mr. Bean replied. "Even driving at a dangerously fast rate of speed, we could not hope to arrive before dusk. It is most unfortunate, but my tardi-ness could not be prevented. Furthermore, it is not at all necessary, sir, for you to see the mine. You have the assayer's report. That assay, sir, if I may be emphatic, is the important factor in our transaction."

Mr. Fleming sighed. "Well, I guess you're right. But to tell you the truth, Bean, I don't like your attitude. It seems to me that you've been trying to give me the good old run-around for the past few months. Your fa-ther, in his business relationships with me, was never evasive. Frankly, I'm beginning to regret that I was fool-ish enough to do business with you by mail. And I should have arranged with my own lawyer to have the title searched."

Mr. Bean pursed his lips primly and pushed his glasses farther up the bridge of his long nose. "Are you implying, sir, that you have not perfect faith in my integrity?"

Mr. Fleming patted his white mustache. "Not exactly, Bean. Everything seems to be in order. But that's just it. It only *seems* to be. Why hasn't your lawyer gotten in touch with me?"

"That question," Mr. Bean said with a shrug of his bony shoulders, "I have answered innumerable times during our correspondence. My father's lawyer has been out of town. Furthermore, it is not at all unusual for several months to elapse while the title to a piece of property is being searched. You yourself, sir, instructed me that I must be absolutely certain that there are no liens."

"Words, words, words!" Mr. Fleming exploded. "I tell you what, Bean, I'm sick and tired of your flimsy excuses. This is final. I'll stop over in Tucson on my way back to Chicago in a week or ten days. I'll notify you in advance of the exact date and hour. You will meet me right here with your lawyer and the deed and we'll close the deal. Otherwise the whole thing is off!" He snatched up his overcoat and suitcase and strode out of the waiting room, followed closely by the gangling Mr. Bean.

Cherry stared after them through the glass partition. It was none of her business, but she couldn't help feeling sorry for the tall, gaunt-faced young man who was apparently pleading so desperately for more time.

"With that build," Cherry said to herself, "Mr. String

Bean must have to have all of his clothes made to order."
She knew that custom-made suits were fabulously expensive and the one he was wearing now was shiny with
age. He probably needed money badly, and she hoped
for his sake that the "deal," whatever it was, would go
through.

Then, as her eyes wandered anxiously upward to the
big clock, she dismissed the two men from her mind.
She had been waiting half an hour. What *could* have
happened to Kirk?

"Miss Ames?" A tall, tanned man had stopped beside
her and with a broad grin was lifting his big cowboy hat.
Folding it across his bright green shirt, he bowed deeply.
"I'm Torry, foreman of the Twin Mounds Ranch,
ma'am. Dr. Monroe was called away on an emergency.
Will I do?" He was in full cowboy regalia: batwing
chaps trimmed with silver; cuffs to match, boots, spurs,
and a gay neckerchief.

Cherry liked him at once. "You certainly will do, Mr.
Torrington," she said as they shook hands. "I was beginning to get sort of scared. A taxi ride out to the ranch
would cost a fortune, wouldn't it?"

"No need for that," he said as he took her bag and
coat. "The station wagon's out in the parking lot. I
came in soon as I got word from Doc. He says, 'You can't
miss her, Torry. The purtiest gal in the whole Yew-
nited States.'" He put her bag in the back and helped

her into the front seat of the station wagon. "And I do believe, ma'am, he didn't exaggerate one morsel."

Cherry laughed. "You know perfectly well, Mr. Torrington, that you knew who I was because of my initials on my suitcase. And please don't call me ma'am. My name is Cherry."

"And mine is Torry," he said as he started the car. "We're friendly folks out here, and don't go for last names much. That is, *most* of us are friendly. I may as well not get used to the idea of calling you Cherry, because soon enough I'll be calling you Calammy, short for Calamity Jane."

"But why?" Cherry asked. "Did a black cat just run in front of the car?"

He shook his head. "You shore are walking into an unlucky setup, ma'am. Those Longman twins—Johnny and Jacqueline! I don't have any trouble with 'em myself because they like to ride and I don't hand out hosses to dudes who disobey orders. And Harold Bean—he's the tutor—he don't have no trouble with 'em either, 'cause he let's 'em do just as they please. But the nurses, now, 'pears like they can't take them ornery twins—nor that ornery Mrs. Blair. Can't say that I blame 'em, either. We haven't had a nurse stay at the ranch longer than a month since the season opened last fall. If you last two weeks I'll eat my boots, spurs and all."

"Oh, dear," Cherry said, "it can't be as bad as all that.

I'm used to wacky teen-agers. My next-door neighbor, Midge Fortune, is always getting into scrapes. And as for cranky patients, I'm used to them, too. Sick people are apt to be cranky."

"The tutor himself," he continued gloomily, just as though she hadn't said anything, "is no prize. Just looking at Harold Bean gives me goose pimples. Six feet four without his boots, and he doesn't weigh much more than you do, ma'am, I'll wager. The human skeleton— Ichabod Crane in person. Uriah Heep in personality. Why he—"

"Harold Bean?" Cherry interrupted in amazement. "Why, I saw him while I was waiting at the terminal. He was late for a business appointment with a man who flew on the same plane with me from Chicago."

"I think you must be mistaken, ma'am," the foreman said. "The human string bean doesn't have business appointments with anybody. He's definitely the scholarly type."

"But I couldn't have been mistaken," Cherry argued. "I distinctly heard Mr. Fleming call him Harold Bean, and there just couldn't be two people with the same name and the same unusual physical characteristics. I don't know anything about his personality, of course, but I felt sorry for him. I got the impression that Mr. Fleming wants to back out of some real-estate transaction which Harold Bean is handling for him. I also couldn't help getting the impression from the rather threadbare clothes the tutor was wearing that he isn't exactly rich."

"Hasn't a thin dime," the foreman agreed.

"Is he land-poor then?" Cherry asked. "I mean, does he own property on which there is valuable ore but hasn't enough money to mine it?"

The foreman chuckled. "He's land-poor all right, if by that you mean he doesn't own a square inch of desert sand. At least, that's what the Conrads told me. They knew his father well and should know his financial status. But why Harold Bean works at the ranch for chicken feed when he could get twice as much at one of the boarding schools is beyond me. Course, he's supposed to be writing a thesis for his Ph.D., but I can't say that the clackety-clack of his typewriter keeps anyone awake nights. But many a night have I been wakened out of a sound sleep by the clackety-clack of his midget car as he rattles past the bunkhouse on his way back from Tucson. So you could be right, ma'am," he finished. "If folks own land on which there is valuable ore they're apt to keep it a secret until said land is sold to the highest possible bidder."

Cherry nodded. "And as to his driving into Tucson at night, why there's nothing mysterious about that. He's probably doing research. You can't write a thesis without first getting some material. As *you* well know, Mr. Torrington. I happen to know from a letter Mrs. Conrad wrote me that you're a college graduate yourself. So please stop calling me ma'am."

He roared with laughter. "I ought to brush up on my cowboy lingo for you dudes. But seriously, Cherry, this job is not going to be an easy one. I don't think Monroe has the faintest idea of what goes on. He only comes out on Monday mornings—unless somebody has an attack, which, with the exception of Mrs. Blair who is always on the verge of or just recovering from one, seldom happens. Señora copes with Mrs. Blair and only calls the doctor when it gets so bad she needs oxygen. When Señora is not there, you'll cope with Blair, and you may as well know right now that you're licked before you've started. With the exception of Señora, nurses in Mrs. Blair's opinion are not Florence Nightingales. They're Lucrezia Borgias. And the Longman twins are about as fond of nurses as they are of black widow spiders. Those two kids are about as friendly as rattlesnakes. The last nurse tossed in her cap after they filled her bed with lizards."

Cherry couldn't help feeling let down. Perhaps this assignment wasn't going to be a holiday after all. Hard work she wouldn't have minded, but Torry seemed to be trying to warn her about something indefinable. She stared at the awesome chain of mountains, watching the colors change as the sun set. Never had she seen such colors: lavender, purple, orange, vermilion, red. Every color in the rainbow was represented, and many, many more that were never seen in the average rainbow.

Now that they had left the outskirts of Tucson behind them the air was growing cold. Cherry was glad she had worn a sweater with her suit and for additional warmth she draped her coat around her legs. She shivered and said:

"I may become a Calamity Jane, but you certainly are the original Gloomy Gus."

His broad shoulders shook with silent laughter. "I don't want to discourage you, Cherry. You may fool us all. Your doctor beau seems to think that there isn't much you can't accomplish, but I think he should have warned you about some of the complications." He turned the station wagon sharply to the left. "This is our private driveway which is only five miles long. Desert on the left and desert on the right. A cheerful sight, no? When things get too bad, don't try to run away."

Cherry tossed her dark curls. "I have no intention of running away."

"Now you can see the real sunset," he said, chuckling. "What you were admiring before was the reflection in the eastern sky. Fabulous, isn't it?"

The western horizon was, indeed, so fabulous that Cherry could only nod wordlessly. The mountains were deep, dark-purple mounds, contrasting sharply with the almost blinding colors above them. As she watched, the burning red ball of the sun disappeared and slowly the colors became muted. Orange became ocher; reds turned to golden pink—all was pastel. And then, as they dipped down a draw in the driveway, she saw the ranch house. It was a one-story, Spanish-style building of adobe bricks, coated over with stucco. The rusty-red tile roof was silhouetted against the sky, and the big wooden butts which supported the roof and protruded beyond it cast blue-black shadows on the path that led from the driveway to the patio.

Torry parked the car. "It's beautiful," Cherry cried as he helped her climb out. "It makes me feel as though I were a tiny speck in a gorgeous framed landscape."

He lifted her bag from the station wagon. "Just re-member one thing, Calammy. All is not gold that glit-ters!"

CHAPTER II

Patty's Problem

BEFORE CHERRY REACHED THE PATIO, THE DOUBLE glass doors from the ranch house opened, and there, framed on the threshold, was one of the most beautiful women she had ever seen. She held out slim, brown arms to Cherry and said:

"I'm Señora, Miss Ames, and I'm so sorry you were kept waiting at the airport." She was wearing a dirndl skirt that seemed to reflect all of the colors in the sunset, and the sandals on her bare feet were multicolored, too. Over the shoulders of her white batiste peasant blouse she had carelessly placed a crimson sweater. Huge earrings to match twinkled in her small ears, and they were also the exact color of her finger-and-toenail polish. Her sleek black hair was pulled severely back into a huge figure eight that looked as though it were held together with only two hairpins. But Cherry shrewdly guessed at once that nothing short of a hurricane could blow a single strand loose. During the brief minute that they stood on the patio, smiling at each other, Cherry realized that Señora's informal appearance was a studied carelessness.

Cherry had felt let down before, but now sudden shyness made her feel hopelessly lost. "How do you do, Mrs. Conrad?" she stammered.

Señora crossed the patio with quick light steps and seized both of Cherry's hands. "My dear," she said warmly, "you mustn't call me anything but Señora. And don't look so frightened." She frowned over Cherry's shoulder at Torry. "Torry Torrington! You've been scaring this poor child with your tall tales." She tucked Cherry's cold hand through the crook of her arm. "Come along with me, Miss Ames, and I'll show you your room. Torry, bring the suitcase and stop grinning like a baboon. Come along, Miss Ames—no, I'm going to call you Cherry."

She led Cherry into a huge living room which at first glance, because of the picture windows and double doors, seemed more like a glassed-in porch. On the east and west sides of the long room and facing each other were two enormous fireplaces in which logs crackled. There were Indian rugs everywhere: on the old Spanish-tile floor, hanging on the walls, and draped on the large leather couches. An especially bright rug lay across the grand piano. Cherry caught a glimpse of framed landscapes done in flaming colors but none of these was as flamboyantly beautiful as the view from the picture windows. Through them she could see the mountains splashed with the splendor of the setting sun.

"This was the original ranch house," Señora was saying. "My grandfather built it, you know. The guest cottages came much, much later. All of your patients, if you want to call them that, occupy rooms or suites that open into the living room, and all of them are connected to the intercom you can see on the table in the center of the room." She laughed. "I don't mean that they are always connected up to the system, but with a flick of a finger they *can* be. It makes the asthmatics feel more secure, you know. Each one has a little brass dinner bell, too."

Cherry nodded. She knew that asthma sufferers must always be made to feel as secure as possible, for when an attack started, their condition was greatly aggravated by fright.

Señora opened a door. Torry placed Cherry's suitcase inside a tiny room, then with an elaborate bow departed. "It's the size of a cell," Señora said as she drew Cherry into the room. "But charming, don't you agree?"

"It's lovely," Cherry replied. The whitewashed walls

were sharply contrasted by the dark walnut of the base-boards, window trim, and doors. The tiles in the floor were cobalt blue, lemon yellow, scarlet, and chocolate brown—exactly like the tiles in the living room. All of the furniture was roughhewn walnut which had been rubbed with white lead to give a silvery-gray effect, and with the exception of the bed, all of the furniture was built-in. Stenciled on the slab back of a chair that looked as though it might have been an early American New England antique were bright cactus blossoms and the spiky leaves of a yucca plant with its lovely lilies.

Señora pulled the drawstring cord of the monk's-cloth draperies and covered the double glass doors that opened onto the patio. "This is where you sleep," she said. "The Nurse's Station is on the opposite side of the living room. You share this tiny bath with Patty Doake, and I really must apologize for the closet. It's much too tiny, but there are two roomy closets in the Nurse's Station, and you can keep as many of your personal things in there as you like."

"Thank you," Cherry said. "But I can easily put all of the clothes I brought with me in the closet and the bureau drawers. I imagine you'll want me to be in uniform most of the time."

It was more of a question than a statement and Señora shrugged. "When you are on duty, yes. Personally, I wouldn't want you to wear your uniform at all. But some of the older guests—Mrs. Blair, for instance— well, they don't even like *me* to take their temperatures unless I'm in white. I don't know whether I wrote you this or not, but one of us must take the temperature, pulse, and respiration of the ten guests who live here in the hacienda before breakfast and before dinner every day. When you are on duty, you will wear your uni- form, and, of course, when you make the rounds with Dr. Monroe on Monday mornings. And naturally, if anyone needs nursing care. But otherwise, Cherry dear, so far as I am concerned, you may wear anything you like. Blue jeans and a T-shirt—except at dinner. We do dress then—not in formal evening clothes, but semi- formal."

Cherry opened her suitcase and took from the top a cotton frock with a long, full skirt and a bolero jacket. "Will this be all right?" she asked.

"Perfect," Señora cried approvingly.

"But it's the only one I brought with me," Cherry wailed. "Outside of it and the suit I'm wearing I brought nothing but uniforms and riding clothes."

Señora's heavy black eyebrows drew together in a frown. "But, my dear, this is a *guest* ranch. I thought I made it quite plain in my letter that you would act in the capacity of a co-hostess with me! I specifically stated that you would eat at the teen-age table. I really can't imagine why you brought only one evening frock."

"It *was* stupid of me," Cherry admitted ruefully. In her closet at home were several informal dresses which Midge Fortune had urged her to bring. But Cherry, thinking that she would be in uniform most of the time, had ignored Midge. "I'm sorry," she said to Señora contritely. "I'll send an air-mail letter to my mother right away and ask her to send me some more dresses like this one."

"Fine," Señora said, but in a tone of voice which meant to Cherry's sensitive nerves, "See that you do." She left then with: "Dinner is at eight."

Cherry sank down on the bed, wishing more than ever that she had followed Midge's advice. And then the door on the far side of the little bathroom opened and a pretty young girl came into Cherry's room.

"I shouldn't barge in like this without knocking," she said with a shy smile. "But I'm sort of a roommate of yours and I couldn't help hearing what Señora said. Señora doesn't mean to be so—so brisk. Or do I mean, brusque? What I really mean, Miss Ames, is—oh, I have dozens of dinner dresses you can borrow. We're about the same size, except that you're an inch or so taller, but we can easily let out the hems."

"How darling of you!" Cherry cried. "But I don't think I have any right to borrow your dresses. It was silly of me not to realize that at a guest ranch I'd be expected to dress up a bit for dinner. And I don't blame Señora at all for being disappointed in me." She smiled at the pretty little teen-ager. "You must be Patty Doake?"

"That's right," Patty said. "And you must borrow my dresses. That's one thing I do have plenty of—clothes. You see, I used to live in the big suite the Longman twins have now. But then when Daddy died last summer it turned out that he didn't leave me a cent." Her dark-blue eyes clouded with tears when she spoke of her father.

"I'm sorry," Cherry said softly. "You must miss him terribly."

"I do," Patty said. "And you mustn't think I mind being poor. It's just that it seems so strange. Daddy always said I'd never have to worry about money. He had it all planned so I could go to a college prep school last fall, although I didn't really want to go to college. I want to be a nurse, you see."

"It's just about the most satisfying profession in the world," Cherry said. "A lot of nurses are college graduates, Patty, but a high school diploma is all you need in order to enter a nursing school."

"I know," Patty said. "But I won't get a high school diploma. I'll be sixteen in May and then I can get my working papers. I'll have to get a job right away. I can't keep on living here after that. Not unless Señora hires me as a full-time maid. And she'll never do that. She doesn't like me to do the work I do now, which isn't very much. I make beds and dust and help out in the kitchen."

"That sounds like a lot," Cherry said. "Especially if you have classes in the morning and study periods in the afternoon and evening. You should have some rest and outdoor exercise, too."

"That's what Señora says," Patty agreed. "She and Uncle Frank wanted to adopt me when Daddy died. But I know they only said that because they felt sorry for me. Although I really am their daughter in a way. This is the only home I've ever known. My mother died when I was just a baby, and Daddy brought me here so Señora could take care of me. He was away a lot of the time on business trips that took him all over the world. I hardly knew him until five years ago when he and Mr. Bean came back from South America."

Cherry had been shaking the wrinkles out of her uniforms before she hung them in the closet. She stopped and stared over one shoulder at Patty. "Bean? Isn't that the tutor's name?"

Patty nodded. "Harold Bean's father and Daddy were sort of partners. I never knew exactly what their business was, but they always had plenty of money. Daddy never left Tucson without giving the Conrads a huge check so I could have everything I wanted, and he sent me wonderful presents, too. And when he came back from South America he said he had brought a nest egg for me. Daddy had to go to work when he was my age, so he didn't finish high school. I guess that's why he was so determined that I would have a college education."

"I can understand that," Cherry said. "But what happened to the nest egg, Patty?"

"I don't know." Patty twisted a strand of her dark hair around one slim finger. "Sometimes, Miss Ames, I think it must be hidden out in The Castle somewhere. But I've searched and searched. There's nothing there of any value. The property isn't worth anything, either. It's just an acre of land out on the desert ten miles from here, in the foothills. And The Castle itself is—well, so queer, nobody would want to live in it."

"The Castle?" Cherry repeated. "I don't understand, Patty. I'm afraid you'll have to begin at the beginning." She chuckled. "I'm all confused. One minute you tell me you're poor, and in the next breath you imply that you own a castle."

Patty laughed. "You couldn't be any more confused than I am. And it isn't really a castle. It's a strange-looking house which Daddy and Mr. Bean built on a pie-shaped foundation right after they came back from South America. They bought the acre of land from the Conrads and built the house themselves."

"Oh," Cherry interrupted, remembering the conversation Harold Bean had had that afternoon with Mr. Fleming in the airport terminal. "Maybe that acre of land is valuable, Patty. I mean, is there a mine on it? And, if so, wouldn't Harold Bean, as his father's sole heir, have a half interest in it?"

Patty shook her head. "The answer to both questions is no. There's nothing on the land but The Castle, and it belongs to me. It took Daddy and Mr. Bean a year to finish it, and then they moved out there to live. But Mr. Bean didn't stay long. He turned over his share to Daddy and went off on a business trip. A year later he died somewhere in Alaska. I was only twelve then, so I don't know what happened to him. Although Mr. Bean was Daddy's best friend, I hardly ever saw him or Harold who was a junior at the University when his father died." She stared down at her hands which she had tensely folded in her lap. "I didn't really know my own father, Miss Ames. When he came back from South America and said he wasn't ever going to go away again, I thought we'd get to know each other. But that first year he spent most of the time with Mr. Bean building The Castle, and they never let a single solitary soul come near the place. Then when it was finished he moved out there with a lot of books on poetry and philosophy and I hardly ever saw him after that. He didn't have any visitors—not even me. About once a week he'd drive along the old wagon road in his jalopy—the one I sold Torry—and spend the day with me. And when he left, right up until the very end, he would always say:

" 'You have nothing to worry about, Patty. I'll never let anything happen to your nest egg.' "

Patty said nothing for several minutes and Cherry couldn't think of a word to say. Mr. Doake, in Cherry's opinion, sounded as though he must have been very eccentric. The nest egg may well have been a figment of his imagination. Cherry unpacked her toilet articles and began to put framed snapshots of her father and mother and Charlie and Midge and Dr. Joe on her bureau and dressing table. She knew she ought to say something to encourage Patty who was sitting so forlornly on the edge of the bed, but what was there to say? If only there were some tactful way of changing the subject.

Then Cherry had an idea. In her suitcase, wrapped in a red sweater, was a group picture of the Spencer Club which had been taken in front of their apartment, No. 9, in New York City's Greenwich Village. Instead of placing this framed photograph on her bureau she handed it to Patty.

"This is my gang," she said. "We call ourselves the Spencer Club because we were all in the same class at the Spencer Hospital Nursing School."

"What darling uniforms!" Patty cried as she stared admiringly at the seven young nurses who, arms entwined, were obviously posing for the first time in brand-new Visiting Nurse uniforms. "How I envy you, Miss Ames. Please tell me all about you and your friends."

Cherry laughed and sat beside her on the bed. "I can't tell you *all* about us now. There isn't time before dinner. Just to tell you about some of the adventures we had as student nurses would take hours and hours."

"Oh, yes, there is time," Patty pleaded. "I mean, time for you to tell me *something* about how it feels to be in training. Not," she added miserably, "that I'll go to a nursing school myself."

Cherry patted her hand. "You mustn't be so discouraged, Patty. If you really think there might be a nest egg hidden out at your castle, I'll help you look for it."

Patty's dark-blue eyes widened. "Will you, Miss Ames? Honest and truly? Dr. Monroe told us all that you're a wonderful detective and that you've solved all sorts of mysteries. I think it must be wonderful to be a nurse *and* a detective."

"I'm not really a detective," Cherry said, smiling. "It so happens that a lot of my patients have had problems which I was lucky enough to be able to help them solve. Just giving bed baths and taking temperatures isn't all there is to nursing, you know. People who are worried don't respond very well to medical treatment. It helps them to relax if you listen sympathetically to their troubles while you're making their beds or giving them an alcohol rub."

Patty nodded. "And you're the kind of person it's easy to talk to. When I came in here I didn't mean to tell you my troubles. I wanted to meet you, of course, because you're a nurse, but mainly I wanted to make you feel at home. I could tell by the sound of her voice that Señora was in one of her snooty moods. She gets that way sometimes, although she's really a very warm person. She's very fussy about certain things, but a lot of other things that bother most people don't bother her at all. I love her, Miss Ames, and I wanted to tell you that, but before I knew it, I was moaning about the fact that I can't go in training."

"Didn't your father ever give you any hint as to what the nest egg was?" Cherry asked. "Or where he kept it? Didn't he leave a will?"

Patty shook her head. "He didn't need to make out a will because I'm his only living relative. I'm not only an orphan, Miss Ames, but I haven't even got a very distant cousin."

She looked so bleak that Cherry felt anger surging through her. Mr. Doake certainly should have made some provision for his lonely young daughter before he died. Especially since he had apparently been a very rich man once. "I just don't believe it," she said, speaking out loud without realizing it. "Your father must have left you some money, Patty. Enough to see you through nursing school, anyway. What did his lawyer say?"

"Mr. Dawson explained it all to me and the Conrads," Patty said, "and it's really very simple. Daddy invested a lot of money in stocks on Wall Street and made a lot more money that way. Then all of a sudden the stocks went down. The Wall Street firm sent Mr. Dawson a telegram saying that if Daddy didn't send them ten thousand dollars right away he would lose everything. Mr. Dawson went right out to The Castle and—and—" Patty swallowed hard. "And found that Daddy had died in his sleep the night before. No one knew that there was anything wrong with his heart . . ." She brightened suddenly. "But that's the way he always said he wanted to go: with his boots on. And I'm really glad for his sake, too, that he didn't know about that telegram from Wall Street."

Cherry frowned. "But your nest egg couldn't have been those stocks, Patty, because your father was obviously speculating—gambling. Your father wouldn't have gambled with money which he had set aside so he could be sure that you would have a college education. Didn't he at least leave you a letter?"

"Oh, yes," Patty cried, springing to her feet. "Under his pillow they found a letter to me with the key to The Castle. I thought for a long time that there might be some clues in the letter, but I couldn't find a one. If you'll wait a minute I'll get it."

She darted through the bathroom into her cubbyhole and in less than a minute was back again. "Oh, Miss Ames," she gasped. "It's gone!"

~~~~~~

CHAPTER III

Unknown Enemies

"ARE YOU SURE IT'S GONE, PATTY?" CHERRY ASKED incredulously. "Where did you keep your father's letter?"

"In a small brown Manila envelope with the key to The Castle," Patty said tearfully. "And I always kept the envelope in my bed-table drawer because I usually reread Daddy's letter before I go to sleep at night. It was there last night. Oh," she interrupted herself, "that's when it was stolen."

"Stolen?" Cherry repeated. "But who would take your father's letter, Patty?"

"I don't know," Patty admitted. "But last night I woke up all of a sudden. I was almost positive that I heard a stealthy sound, like someone closing a door. I was so scared for a moment I could hardly breathe, then I turned on the light. Nobody was in my room but I had the feeling that someone had been there only a minute or so before. After a while I decided I must have been dreaming and went back to sleep."

"I'm sure you were dreaming," Cherry said. "My door to the adjoining bath and your door to the living room were locked, weren't they?"

Patty shook her head. "Señora won't let any of the asthmatics or the teen-agers lock their rooms when they're inside. The doors are very thick and the locks are not easy to break. If an asthmatic had a sudden attack and the door was locked—well, I don't have to explain that rule to *you*. Anyway, nobody locks his or her doors around here. Uncle Frank keeps some of the guests' valuables in the office safe, but most people leave their jewelry lying around in plain view and never worry."

"Well, then," Cherry said cheerfully, "if jewelry isn't stolen you can be sure your envelope is safe, Patty. Some time since you last saw it you may have absent-mindedly put it in your desk or one of your bureau drawers. I'd help you look now, but there's barely time for me to shower and change before dinner."

"But, Miss Ames—"

Cherry interrupted her with a quick hug. "My name is Cherry to you from now on, honey. We'll find the envelope after dinner. I don't go on duty until tomorrow morning at eight, so we can have a real gabfest this evening."

Patty brightened then and hurried into her own room. Cherry had just finished dressing when Señora knocked.

"I'm early," she said apologetically, "but I do want to introduce you to Mr. Conrad and some of the guests before the dinner gong."

Cherry liked Frank Conrad at once. He greeted her with a broad grin that seemed to spread all over his tanned face as he shook her hand with a firm grip that almost hurt. He was not much taller than Señora, but Cherry could see that under his white dinner jacket he had the powerful shoulders of an All-American center. Harold Bean was just exactly the opposite. As Torry had said, he did indeed look so much like Ichabod Crane that Cherry had to suppress a chuckle when she shook hands with him.

"Delighted, I'm sure," he said with an awkward bow. "Welcome to Twin Mounds Ranch."

"Thank you," Cherry said with a warm smile. "It's too bad, Mr. Bean, that I didn't know who you were when I saw you at the airport terminal this afternoon. If I had, I would have introduced myself and asked you to drive me out here I expected Dr. Monroe to meet my plane, you know, and when he didn't show up I got rather nervous."

He blinked his eyes and pushed his glasses farther up

the bridge of his long nose. "You are mistaken, Miss Ames. I was nowhere in the vicinity of the airport today. When your plane arrived, and for an hour thereafter, I was at the library completely absorbed in research work for my thesis."

Cherry grinned cheerfully and blinked her own dark eyes rapidly. After all, it was none of her business, and if the tutor didn't want anyone to know that he *had* met Mr. Fleming in the waiting room that afternoon she would not give away his secret. "The rarefied air out here," she said good-naturedly, "must have played tricks on my eyes. I saw someone who looked enough like you to have been your double." Señora was bringing the Longman twins up to be introduced and Cherry added with a chuckle, "Does everyone out here have a double?"

"John and Jacqueline," Señora said, "this is Miss Ames, the new nurse."

They were identical twins, and if they had been dressed alike, Cherry couldn't have told them apart, for Jacqueline's thick, jet-black curly hair was cut as short as her brother's. They were extraordinarily good-looking, too, with bold, black eyes and red lips that were curled into saucy smiles as they said in unison:

"Hello, nurse."

They pronounced the word *nurse* as an arrogant queen in bygone days would have said "slave," so

Cherry knew at once that these two had no respect for her profession. She started to say "I'm a twin, too," but they had turned their backs on her before she could open her mouth.

The other teen-agers, Nancy, Richie, and Davie, came up then and greeted her politely but with frank disinterest. They hurried outside to join the Longman twins in the patio. Then Señora led Cherry across the room to the west fireplace around which several older men and women had gathered.

"You can only meet four of your five adult patients now," Señora said, "because Mrs. Blair has decided to remain in bed. Tomorrow morning when you take her temperature will be soon enough for you to meet her, my dear. She is the asthmatic to end all asthmatics. A hypochondriac of the first water, and a malingerer whenever she decides that it would be more pleasant to have meals in bed than to bother with dressing."

Before Cherry had a chance to make a reply she was rapidly introduced to Mr. Neap, Mrs. Taper, Mrs. Bloch, and Mr. Caudle. They were all pleasant but so nondescript that so far as connecting their names with their faces was concerned she felt that the introductions had been a waste of time. Then the gong sounded and in a few minutes they were all crowding into the dining room. It was Patty who thoughtfully guided Cherry to her place at the foot of the teen-age table.

"Don't worry about trying to remember names, Miss Ames—Cherry," she said in a low voice as she sat beside her. "I'll tell you who everyone is all over again. I don't know the guests who live in the cabins very well, but the ones you'll have to take care of I've known most of my life. Mr. Neap, Mrs. Taper, Mrs. Bloch, and Mr. Caudle have been spending the winters out here ever since I can remember. And Mrs. Blair, who is the only one who ever has really severe attacks, lives here eight months of the year. She's a terror, but don't you worry. When she's really and truly sick, Dr. Monroe always gets special nurses for her."

"Thank you, Patty," Cherry said gratefully.

The dining room was almost as large as the living room with double glass doors that flanked the patio on the south side. Cherry guessed that the picture windows here faced the east so that the guests could enjoy the beauty of the sunrise in the morning at breakfast. She glanced around curiously.

Not only was the room literally swarming with guests seeking their tables, but intermingling with them were at least a dozen Mexican girls who were bearing trays of glasses filled with ice water and tomato juice. As the ungainly tutor passed them, they somehow deftly swerved in the right direction, thus avoiding catastrophe. At last, after what seemed to Cherry like a series of narrow escapes, he folded himself into his chair opposite her.

Cherry turned to Jacqueline Longman and said with a smile, "I'm a twin, too, you know."

Jacqueline stared at her with a disbelieving expression on her face, but John leaned forward with a friendly grin and asked:

"Really and truly, Miss Ames?"

"Cross my heart and hope to die," Cherry said. "My twin brother's name is Charlie. We come from a small town in Illinois, and he's a student at State Engineering College."

"Is that so?" Harold Bean, who like many thin people had an enormous appetite, had been too busy eating until then to speak. "Excellent, excellent," he said pompously. "At one time I thought of majoring in engineering myself, but since I apparently have the knack of imparting my knowledge to others, I thought it best to major in literature and become a college professor so I can share my knowledge of the classics with others who are not so well read, and who, deplorably, have not my innate ability to absorb what they read. Furthermore—"

John interrupted with a groan. "Never mind, Harold. We know, we know. Thank goodness *you're* not a twin. The State of Arizona couldn't stand two such geniuses." He turned to Cherry. "Tell us more about you and your brother, Charlie. Did you and he have any trouble when you were in school? Because you were twins, I mean."

Cherry's mouth was full, but she chewed and swallowed quickly. The whole atmosphere at the table had changed. The teen-agers had ignored her presence before, but they were now eating quietly, waiting for her reply with obvious interest. Cherry was very hungry and the Mexican dish, whatever its name was, was delicious. But she immediately decided that it was more important for her to satisfy the youngsters' curiosity than to appease her appetite.

"We certainly did," she told John. "For a long time I felt that if Charlie answered questions in class and got good marks in exams, I didn't have to do anything but stare out of the window and dream. And he felt the same way about me. Finally the principal of the school put us in separate classes with different teachers. From then on we had to be on our own. We didn't like it at first, but we're glad it happened now." She grinned. "We couldn't have got very far sharing one diploma."

John threw back his head and roared with laughter. "Now I know for sure that you really are a twin. The same thing is true of us, except that we've never been separated. Since Jackie doesn't care whether she gets even half of a diploma, she dreams all day during classes. Isn't that true?" he asked the tutor.

"Unfortunately, yes," Harold Bean said, pursing his loose-lipped mouth.

"You both make me sick and tired," Jacqueline said.

"How can anyone help falling asleep in classes with a tutor as dull as Harold Bean? Yackitty-yackitty-yackitty! Who cares about algebra anyway?"

"Moreover," the tutor continued, just as though she hadn't interrupted, "if Jacqueline hadn't formed an unfortunate attachment for a certain uncouth cowboy whose given name is the same as that of the immortal bard she would be a brilliant scholar. Furthermore—"

"I won't stand for it. I won't." Jacqueline jumped up, knocking over her chair. "How dare you accuse me of being in love with a common cowboy? Why, the only times I ever speak to Bill are when he saddles and bridles my horse." Her voice ended in a choking cough.

Cherry quickly slipped out of her place and hurried around the table to her. "Calm down, honey," she said soothingly. "It isn't good for you to get excited or angry. Your brother and Mr. Bean were just teasing. My brother teases the daylights out of me from morning to night. I know how annoying it is. Just pay no attention to them and sit down and finish your dinner."

Harold Bean, in his clumsy way, was now standing on the other side of the angry, choking girl. Nervously he pushed his horn-rimmed glasses farther up the bridge of his nose. "My dear Jackie," he said in his nasal voice. "My dear, sweet girl. Pray forgive my insufferable loquacity. As Miss Ames said, I was merely being nonsensical."

Jacqueline gave him a wordless but scathing glance and turned away from him to grab Cherry's arm. "I feel as though an attack were coming on," she gasped. "I want to go to bed. Will you fix it so that my head is higher than my feet?"

Cherry led her quickly to the patio and into the living room.

"Stop worrying, Jackie," she said gently. "You're not going to lose your breath. You're going to feel fine as soon as I make you comfortable in bed. Where is your suite, honey?"

With one hand on her throat, and with the other curled tightly in the crook of Cherry's arm, Jacqueline led the way across the living room. She opened the bedroom door herself, switched on the light, and collapsed on the attractive walnut bed. It didn't look at all like an old-fashioned hospital bed, but Cherry quickly found the crank and turned it, so that in another minute Jacqueline's head was higher than her feet and her knees were raised slightly. Her face had been flushed with anger before, but now it was pale. Her pulse and respiration were rapid.

To make matters worse she began to cry.

"Stop it," Cherry said sharply. She knew that if Jacqueline kept on crying she would soon be choking and coughing and in a few minutes she would lose control of herself. That would mean a shot of adrenalin in a hurry.

"Stop feeling sorry for yourself," Cherry said. "Think about somebody else. Patty Doake, for instance. There's a girl who has a right to cry."

"Patty—hasn't—got asthma," Jacqueline gasped, but she was no longer crying.

"Neither have you," Cherry said with a smile. "You wouldn't have any attacks living out here on this wonderful ranch if you kept your temper under control." She took a quick look at Jacqueline's chart. The doctor's prescription for mild attacks read:

"Give aminophylline suppository every 6–8 hours."

"Are you going to give me a shot?" Jacqueline asked.

"Not now," Cherry said cheerfully, "because you don't need it. Your breathing is slowing down to its normal rate, and so is your pulse." With her fingers on Jacqueline's slim, brown wrist, she continued. "You're an intelligent girl, Jackie Longman. You should have a better understanding of yourself. Any emotion—anger, fear, or sorrow—affects your whole system. Don't let little things annoy you. It isn't worth it. Every attack you have makes you more liable to another one. It's a habit-forming sort of thing. You don't want to end up like Mrs. Blair who apparently has one attack after another."

Jacqueline shuddered and then laughed. "Ugh. Mrs. Blair is just awful. I hate her. I hated all of the other nurses, too. They were all old and ugly and forever preaching. You're different. You say all the same things they said to me, but it doesn't sound like preaching be-cause you're so young and pretty—and, best of all, you're a twin, too."

"I'm nowhere near as pretty as you are," Cherry said. "You and your brother are really and truly very, very handsome."

"Oh, please don't say handsome is as handsome does," Jacqueline interrupted. "Don't let's talk about me and Johnny. Let's talk about you and your brother. Does he really tease you a lot?"

"Frightfully," Cherry said. "But I know he loves me and, goodness knows, I just adore him."

"I adore Johnny, too," Jacqueline said. "I can't stand it when he gets sick or hurt. If he has an attack, it feels worse than if I was having one myself, although I usu-ally do get one if he gets one."

Cherry nodded. "Twins are like that. I'll tell you more about Charlie and me some other time. Right now, Señora is waiting for me. I haven't yet seen the Nurse's Station. I don't know which rooms my patients occupy either, and I go on duty tomorrow morning."

"All right," Jacqueline said. "But I would like to hear more about your brother. Have you got a picture of him?"

"Of course," Cherry said. "It's in a big silver frame on my bureau. Go right in any time you want and look at it." She started to add, "We don't look a bit alike.

Charlie's a lot taller than I am and is as blond as I am dark." But just then the loud-speaker in the living room blared:

"Miss Ames. Nurse Ames. Please report to the office."

"Good-by, Jackie," Cherry said. "I'll see you tomorrow before breakfast unless you need me before then." She hurried out and across the big room to the attractive office. Señora was seated at the huge mahogany desk and she looked very angry.

"I'm sorry I kept you waiting," Cherry said. "Jacqueline Longman got rather upset during dinner, and I thought I had better stay with her until she had calmed down."

"Please be seated, Miss Ames," Señora said coldly. "I understand you were the cause of Jacqueline's fit of temper."

"Me?" Cherry was so surprised that she toppled into the nearest chair.

Señora nodded. "I've been told by reliable witnesses that you teased the child unmercifully. Now, I can understand why you didn't fall in love at first sight with the Longman twins. They are, to be brutally frank, spoiled brats. They are very annoying in every way because they are forever playing pranks. They undoubtedly did something which annoyed you, and so you retaliated by teasing Jackie. I will forgive it this once, but it cannot happen again."

"But I didn't do anything of the kind," Cherry protested.

Señora gracefully waved one slim-fingered hand. "Perhaps you didn't deliberately mean to tease her. Perhaps you were merely being facetious. At any rate, this lecture was probably not necessary. You are surely now fully aware of the fact that Jackie is both supersensitive and overemotional." She suddenly smiled warmly. "I wish we could afford not to have problem children here, but we can't, Cherry. All asthmatics, young or old, are problem children in a way. Half of the time I feel like spanking Jackie and Johnny; often it's hard not to give them a good scolding. And as for Mrs. Blair—!" She shrugged her slim shoulders expressively. "That woman would try the patience of Job. But I have no real worries about you, Cherry. Dr. Monroe recommended you so highly that I'm sure you'll be able to cope beautifully with everything, once you are adjusted."

Cherry was still so bewildered by the unjust accusation that she could only mumble, "Thank you, Señora."

Señora took from the long drawer of the desk a key ring and a floor plan of the hacienda. "You can't begin to get adjusted," she said, "until you're oriented. Why don't you come around and stand beside me while I print on the floor plan the names of the guests who are now occupying the various rooms and suites?"

Cherry did as she was told, but all of a sudden her

eyes were blinded by tears. She had been at the ranch only a few hours and already she had made enemies. For that's what they were: those "reliable witnesses" who had told Señora that she, Cherry Ames, had unmercifully teased Jacqueline Longman.

Who were they? And why were they her enemies?

~~~~~~

CHAPTER IV

A Strange Letter

IT WAS AFTER NINE WHEN CHERRY FINALLY WAS FREE
to go back to her tiny room and relax. She changed into
warm flannel pajamas, because it was really cold now,
and donning her warm housecoat, sat down at her desk
and hastily scribbled a note to her mother:

"Everything is too hectic now," she wrote, "for me to
give you any details. But I stupidly didn't bring any of
those informal dinner dresses which Midge told me I
should bring. Just that one you pressed for me at the
last minute. Darling, could you send me the others as
soon as possible? I'm sending this letter air mail, so I'll
count on getting a big box from you before the week
end."

Cherry sealed the envelope, put an air-mail stamp on

it, and then hesitated. She hadn't had a chance yet to find out about the mailing system at the ranch. Suppose mail was only brought into Tucson once a week and the once-a-week was a Saturday? In that case the only way to solve the problem would be to telephone her mother right away.

Cherry darted through the adjoining bathroom and tapped on Patty Doake's door. "Patty, it's Cherry. May I speak to you for a minute?"

The door was opened so quickly that Cherry knew Patty must have had her hand on the doorknob before she knocked.

"I was just going to come over and call on you," Patty said. "For our gabfest, you know. I was standing here, trying to get up my courage. I know you're tired—the long plane trip . . . your first day . . . and Jackie . . . I should think you'd be on the verge of collapsing."

Cherry grinned. "I am, but first I want to find out where I should put this air-mail letter to my mother so that it'll go off as soon as possible tomorrow. Next, I want to have a cozy chat with you. We'll both sleep better for it. I, because I love to reminisce about the days when I was a student nurse. And you, Patty, because it all seems like a dream to you—a dream which I'm sure will come true someday."

"I hope so." Patty slipped on a quilted robe. "I'll put

your letter in the box for you, Cherry," she said. "You probably didn't notice it when you arrived this afternoon. It's just outside your doors by the path that leads from the driveway to the patio. Torry drives into Tucson every morning with the letters we want to send out and picks up our mail at the same time." She took Cherry's letter and hurried out through her door to the living room and in a minute joined Cherry in her room. "That's that. Now, you get into bed and I'll curl up in the chair."

"Yes, nurse," Cherry said meekly as she obeyed orders. "But I thought we were going to search your room for the missing envelope. Did you find it yourself?"

Patty shook her head. "It isn't there anywhere, Cherry. I've spent the whole evening looking. But let's not talk about that now. Please tell me some of the experiences you had as a student nurse."

"Well," Cherry began, "it's lots of fun and such a challenge! You're awfully scared at first and for a long time afterward, but right off you meet a lot of other probies—probationers, who are just as scared as you are. And everyone, including handsome young interns, are very nice and helpful. When I arrived at Spencer that first day it seemed as huge as a fortress to me. I stood in the rotunda too terrified to move, let alone try to find my way to the T.S.O.—the Training School Office. That's where you report first."

"I'm too scared even to think right now," Patty said as she snuggled under the comforter she had taken off the foot of Cherry's bed. "How soon was it before you met your classmates? The girls in the picture you showed me, I mean."

"I met Ann Evans first," Cherry said, taking the framed photograph from her night table and pointing to Ann. "She's married now and so is Vivian Warren. The plump girl is Bertha Larsen. The last time I saw her was when we were both on duty in the Kentucky mountains. Mai Lee is the lovely Chinese-American nurse and she's the only one of our crowd who is at No. 9 right now. The girl on my right, with the snub nose and freckles, is redheaded Gwen Jones. On the other side of me is Josie Franklin, the shy-looking girl with glasses. They're both at Spencer now taking postgraduate courses. At least they were when I last heard from them. They may have finished by now. I met them all the very first evening, and we sort of banded together after that. The whole place seemed like a labyrinth and we kept getting lost." Cherry chuckled. "We got into all sorts of scrapes, too. Once Gwen and Ann and I borrowed Sally Chase, the demonstration doll, for a little girl on the Private Pavilion. We would have been caught by the Chief Surgeon if the young intern, Jim Clayton, hadn't helped me get the doll back to the classroom in the basement. Take my advice and never borrow a Sally Chase.

They're made of rubber, and when you're scared and in a hurry they're about as easy to handle as a young zeppelin."

"Is that the doll you practice on?" Patty asked.

"At first," Cherry replied. "After you've learned how to make an empty bed, then a bed with the doll in it, you practice making beds with other probationers in it. We gave each other bed baths and took each other's temperatures and all that kind of thing until we were good enough to be really useful on the wards. You don't have ward duty until after a month of instruction, and the first two weeks you don't do much. Then all of a sudden you find that you have mastered the art of not only making beds and taking temperatures, but the giving of hypodermics and applying hot poultices. During my third month I was on the men's surgical ward. One day, to my horror, the great Dr. Wylie ordered me to help him change a dressing. He was surrounded by awed young interns, and I got so rattled I forgot everything I had been taught. He was furious and I was sure I'd never get my cap, but I did."

"It must be terribly exciting to win your cap," Patty said wistfully. "You get new uniforms after that, don't you?"

Cherry nodded. "Off goes the probationer's gray, and you don striped dresses with white bibs and aprons. You learn an awful lot awfully fast after that, and time goes quickly because everything you learn is so interesting. Senior year is the best of all, because you're given more and more responsibility every day and in lots of ways you're treated as though you were a graduate nurse. You assist the obstetrician in the Delivery Room, and care for the mothers before and after their babies are born. And you're assigned to the Nursery where you take care of newborn babies. But the acid test comes in the O.R. —the Operating Room. During the first two years of training you learn how to take care of postoperative patients who are almost ready to be discharged. But in your senior year you're assigned to them when they've only recently come from the O.R., and finally you're assigned to O.R. itself."

"That would scare me to death," Patty said with a wan smile which meant: *Oh, how I wish I could have that experience someday!* "I know I'd do everything all wrong and be the death of the poor patient."

Cherry laughed. "No chance of that. At first you simply get more instructions on surgical instruments; how to sterilize them, how to set up a sterile table, drape the patient, and handle supplies. You're a 'dirty' nurse for a long time, which means you're sort of a messenger girl who goes in and out of O.R. without contaminating anything. And in the very beginning you simply watch operations through the glass of the O.R. amphitheater. The surgeon lectures to student doctors and nurses as he works, and the first operation you witness is usually a simple one. The warming-up process lasts about a week, and the first operation you assist at is a minor one like a tonsillectomy. This second step lasts about a week, too, and you simply assist the nurse. Then you act as first assistant on more difficult operations, and by that time you know the whole routine as well as you do your own name, so you really are calm, cool, and collected."

"You make it sound as simple as A, B, C," Patty said. "I'm sure I'd give the surgeon a pair of scissors when he needed a knife—I mean scalpel." She drew up her knees and clasped her slim, brown hands around them. "No, I don't mean that, Cherry. I'm sure, with enough training, I'd be a good nurse. I've had lots of experience working with Señora. In emergencies, you know, when the resident nurse had just left and the new one hadn't yet arrived. I've done the T.P.R.'s of well patients for her lots of times, and I know how to make beds with miter-corners and give bed baths and alcohol rubs, and I've taken both of the Red Cross First Aid courses and I know that the High Fowler's Position for asthmatics means that you crank the bed so that the patient is in a relaxed sitting position, and that the Semi-Fowler means that the patient's head is raised about as high as though he had two or three pillows and that you always raise their knees enough so that their feet won't touch the footboard of the bed, and I'm used to being around oxygen tanks, too," she went on breathlessly. "I've often put up the sign DANGER! OXYGEN BEING USED. NO OPEN FLAMES. NO SMOKING outside Mrs. Blair's door, because she's forever having attacks and needing oxygen. I understand the gauge, too. It's usually set at ten liters, and before it runs down to zero, you should send for another tank, because *zero* means that there's only enough oxygen left to last for about twenty minutes. And the reason why you don't change tanks until the old one is empty is not only because of the waste, but because oxygen floating around loose is a dangerous thing. Señora worked in a rest home for asthmatics once where there was a faulty electrical fixture and the escaping oxygen caused an explosion. And—" She stopped suddenly as completely out of breath, Cherry thought, as an asthmatic who was suffering from a severe attack.

"My goodness," Cherry said with a grin, "if you've picked up all that knowledge before your sixteenth birthday, you certainly will make a wonderful nurse! Patty, we've just got to find your father's letter and see if there aren't some clues in it. Who could have stolen your brown envelope?"

"Jackie probably," Patty replied. "It would be her idea of a joke. But she'll return it soon because she's usually sorry right after she plays that kind of mean trick. She's not really bad, you know. It's just that she sometimes acts without thinking."

"She's young for her age in lots of ways," Cherry agreed. "But it couldn't have been Jackie if the envelope was taken late last night. None of the teen-agers are allowed to leave their rooms after nine o'clock."

"You don't know Jackie," Patty replied. "She only obeys rules when she feels like it."

"I still don't think she'd take something that didn't belong to her," Cherry argued. "I think you ought to report the theft to Mr. Conrad, Patty."

Patty shook her head. "That would be tattling. Anyway, nothing important was stolen. And I know the letter Daddy wrote me by heart." She took a slip of paper from the pocket of her robe and handed it to Cherry. "Here's a copy I made for you. Maybe you can find some clues in it. To me it seems more like a lecture. I mean, advice on how to be happy and all that sort of thing."

Cherry read the letter aloud:

> *"My darling daughter:*
>   *" 'Early to bed and early to rise*
>   *Makes a man healthy, wealthy, and wise.'*
>   *"Be persevering. Remember that my vaulting ambition was to amass a nest egg for you, and I never let bad luck floor me.*
>   *Your loving father"*

Cherry stopped. Mr. Doake certainly must have been

eccentric. What he had written was good advice, but knowing his daughter's ambition he should have left her some concrete evidence of his love.

"Well, what do you think?" Patty asked hopelessly.

"I don't know what to think," Cherry said. "He does mention the nest egg, so maybe this was his way of assuring you that it is hidden out at The Castle. And he tells you to be persevering, which could mean that if you don't find the nest egg right away you shouldn't give up too easily. What do you yourself think, Patty?"

"At first," Patty said, "I didn't think. I just took it for granted that I'd always have plenty of money because I'd always had everything I wanted and much more. Then when the lawyer, Mr. Dawson, told me that Daddy had lost every cent when the bottom fell out of the stock market, I began to think about the nest egg. I knew Daddy didn't trust banks, so there was no sense in trying to find out if he'd put some money in a savings account or something valuable in a safe-deposit vault. So the only thing to do was to search The Castle. I have looked, Cherry, but there isn't anything there. All of the furniture, except the two sofa beds, is made of cholla cactus wood, so there couldn't be any secret panels in it. The desk, with the bookcases on each side, is one unit —built-in, and attached to the wall studs. All of us, Mr. Dawson and the Conrads and Torry and I have searched the desk and the bookcases a dozen times. The walls are made of adobe brick and the floors are tiled, so they're out as secret hiding places."

"I'm not so sure of that," Cherry objected. "Maybe one or more of the tiles is removable."

Patty shook her head. "We tried every single one. I even took the mattresses and the chair and sofa cushions apart. But maybe when you go out there, Cherry, you'll think of something. You will go, won't you? Next Sunday on your day off?"

"Of course," Cherry said enthusiastically. "I do hope the key is returned by then. I can hardly wait to see The Castle. It sounds like a fascinating place, and—well, I may as well admit it—I *do* love a mystery!"

CHAPTER V

~~~~~~

First Day on Duty

BUT THE NEXT MORNING CHERRY WAS TOO BUSY EVEN
to think about Patty's problem and the Mystery Castle.
Breakfast was at eight o'clock, so she had to chart all
of her patients' T.P.R.'s before then. She started with
the teen-agers, popping a thermometer into each one's
mouth, beginning with the twins. This took about five
minutes, so when she came back to John and Jacqueline
and started all over again, she knew that the thermometer had been in their mouths for the required three minutes. Everyone's temperature, pulse, and respiration was
normal, so she went on to the adults.

"May as well start with the most difficult patient," she
decided as she tapped on Mrs. Blair's door. Opening it
a crack, she said, "It's the nurse, Mrs. Blair. May I come
in and take your temperature?"

"You may," a sepulchral voice replied dismally.

Cherry slipped inside and crossed over to the bed where the elderly woman was resting, her head propped up by three pillows. "Good morning, Mrs. Blair," she said cheerfully. "I'm Miss Ames. I'm sorry I didn't have the pleasure of meeting you last evening." Cherry shook down the thermometer until the mercury stopped at 96 degrees. She had stolen one swift glance at the cross-looking face as she took the thermometer from the glass on the patient's bureau. One glance was enough!

Mrs. Blair was not only an ugly woman, but she was in an ugly mood. She had stiffly waved, straw-colored hair that was streaked with gray, and Cherry was to learn that Mrs. Blair always, day and night, wore it tucked into an auburn net. In Cherry's opinion it made her look as though she were wearing an inverted ice bag. Her faded blue eyes and pale, thin lips were almost lost in the pouting lines that furrowed her face.

"Good morning, Miss Ames," she greeted Cherry in her funereal voice. "I am not at all well. I had a very bad night. You, on the other hand, look the picture of health. I cannot imagine why you feel it necessary to wear rouge. You have obviously had a good night's rest, and you must know that I am very, *very* allergic to all cosmetics."

"I know," Cherry said soothingly. "But I'm not wearing rouge. This is my natural color. It's why I was given

the nickname of Cherry. Don't you worry about anything. Just keep the thermometer under your tongue
until I come back."

Cherry fled. She knew that nothing she said would
ever convince Mrs. Blair that she was not wearing rouge.
To argue the point would only make the patient so irate
that she might work herself up into an attack.

Mr. Neap, Mrs. Taper, Mrs. Bloch, and Mr. Caudle
were all placidly waiting for her in their respective
rooms, with the doors open. They were obviously used
to the routine and outside of greeting her pleasantly,
they said nothing. So according to her wrist watch,
Cherry returned to Mrs. Blair exactly three minutes
after she had left her.

The moment she took the thermometer from the old
woman's mouth, Mrs. Blair said irritably, "You were
gone long enough, nurse. You don't seem to realize that
I am a very ill patient. You should never, *never* leave
me alone with that dangerous instrument in my mouth.
Suppose I had a coughing attack and bit it? Suppose I
had a choking attack and swallowed it?"

Cherry smiled. "Your temperature, pulse, and respiration are normal, Mrs. Blair. I hope you feel up to having
breakfast in the dining room. The view from the picture
windows must be beautiful in the morning." She replaced Mrs. Blair's chart on the hook beside the bed and
started for the door.

"WAIT!"

Cherry stopped, her hand on the doorknob. Anger made her red cheeks flame. No one, sick or well—not even Dr. Wylie in her student nursing days—had ever yelled at her in such a loud, rude voice. Furthermore, no asthmatic with a grain of sense should indulge in such a shriek. Cherry's concern for her patient made her anger leave her as quickly as it had come. She turned and came back to the side of the bed. "Is there anything I can do to make you comfortable, Mrs. Blair?"

"Yes," the old woman said disagreeably. "Raise my knees. Bring me a glass of fresh water. Take away these wretched pillows and raise the head of the bed so that I am in the High Fowler's position. My feet are cold; bring me a hot-water bottle. Have a menu sent in. I shall have breakfast in bed."

Cherry raised Mrs. Blair's knees slightly. "I'm sorry," she said quietly, "but that's all I can do for you right now. Mr. Neap, Mrs. Taper, Mrs. Bloch and Mr. Caudle are all waiting with thermometers in their mouths. As soon as I have attended to their charts I'll come back and carry out your other instructions."

Mrs. Blair spluttered something unintelligible as Cherry hurried away. She returned in five minutes to find that her patient was still spluttering.

"Now," Cherry said brightly, "I can give you all the time you want. I know how you hate being left with the thermometer in your mouth, so I'm sure you're glad that your neighbors are out of their misery."

Gently she removed two of the pillows and raised the head of the bed. In the bathroom she found that there were taps for ice water as well as hot and cold water, so refilling Mrs. Blair's bedside carafe and providing her with a hot-water bottle took scarcely two minutes.

"There," Cherry said as she remade the foot of the bed. "Unless you want anything more, I'll go to the dining room and have a menu sent right in. After breakfast I'll give you a bath and back rub if you like. That is, if there's time before Dr. Monroe arrives."

Mrs. Blair stopped spluttering and glared at Cherry. "Young woman, I shall report you to Dr. Monroe. You may as well pack up your things right away. No nurse —do you understand me?—*no nurse* stays at this ranch unless *I* approve of her. I definitely disapprove of you."

The criticism was so unfair that Cherry's temper flared, but her sense of humor quickly came to her rescue. The whole situation was ludicrous. Mrs. Blair was just one of those patients whom every nurse during her career has to cope with occasionally. No matter how much extra attention you give them they are never satisfied. But because they really were sick, even though a great many of their ills were imagined, you had to make allowances.

"I'm sorry you disapprove of me," Cherry finally said

meekly. "I've tried to make you comfortable, Mrs. Blair."

"You are both competent and efficient, I'll say that for you," Mrs. Blair snapped. "Too much so for my personal comfort. There was no reason for you to leave me once, let alone twice. I am accustomed to having the resident nurse attend to me before she so much as goes near another patient. You will never get on at this ranch if you are going to treat me as though I were a mechanical thing on an assembly line. You are undoubtedly in a hurry because you came here for the sole purpose of getting yourself a husband."

Cherry gasped, speechless with amazement.

"Don't interrupt," Mrs. Blair said, raising one brown-spotted hand. "I know your type. You're young and pretty and your uniform enhances your figure. Dr. Monroe tells me that he met you when you were on duty together on a Caribbean cruise. You have tracked him down to this ranch. You will marry him, willy-nilly. But if he should, by an chance, escape your clutches, you will turn your wiles on the young tutor or the handsome young foreman."

Cherry laughed good-naturedly. "Even if I were an adventuress, Mrs. Blair, you can't believe that I'd want to marry anyone as penniless as poor Mr. Bean."

"Poor, indeed!" Mrs. Blair snorted. "Only last fall he sold some of his father's property for five thousand dollars. I saw the check representing the down payment myself. The envelope containing it was put into my mailbox by mistake. I opened it because I did not realize that it was addressed to Mr. Harold Bean, *not* to Mrs. Harold Blair." She straightened and sitting bolt upright, her back a ramrod, continued:

"Actually, I did not open the envelope, because it was not sealed. The mucilage on the flap had not been sufficiently moistened by the sender. When I read the letter and realized that it and the check were not intended for me, I immediately replaced them, sealed the envelope properly, and put it in the tutor's box."

"Oh," Cherry said mildly, "if the down payment on a purchase agreement was five thousand dollars, Mr. Bean must own some very valuable property. But I assure you, Mrs. Blair, that I wouldn't marry him if he were the richest man in the world." She started for the door.

"I have not finished speaking my mind yet," the old woman shouted. "I have never mentioned that check to anyone because I am not the type who betrays other people's secrets.

"Then why did you tell me about it?" Cherry asked, genuinely amazed.

"Because," Mrs. Blair said, "I knew it would not surprise you to discover that our threadbare tutor is really a wealthy landowner. You undoubtedly made it your business to ascertain his and the foreman's financial status before you accepted this position." She shook her finger at Cherry. "Don't interrupt me, miss. I know your type because I was young once myself. Although you will probably not believe it, I was described as a Titian beauty. I had flaming golden-red hair, a milk-white complexion, and a figure that made all of the great artists in America ask me to pose for them."

"Oh, dear," Cherry thought, as the old woman rambled on and on, "I won't have time for breakfast if she doesn't stop soon. And it's all so silly, but there's no sense in trying to convince her that I didn't come out here to get a husband."

Just then Señora arrived and evidently took in the situation at a glance. "Good morning, Mrs. Blair," she interrupted the flow of words. "I've brought along a menu because I thought perhaps you would like to have breakfast in bed. The baked apples this morning are really delicious. . . ."

Cherry gratefully slipped away. She had barely time for coffee and toast. The doctor would arrive at nine and she must be in the Nurse's Station waiting for him. Señora had given her the key to the station the evening before, so Cherry went straight to that suite from the dining room. The suite consisted of two rooms and a bath. There were roomy closets and cupboards and plenty of shelves. In one room there was a comfortable chair bed with an adjustable back and a plump ottoman for the patient's feet. There were two other overstuffed chairs, a kneehole desk for the doctor, and a stiff-backed chair beside it. In one drawer of the desk was the Doctor's Order Book: a big loose-leaf notebook with separate sheets for each patient, which, after receiving the doctor's orders, Cherry would remove and clip to each patient's chart. Cherry took the book from the drawer, placed it on the desk, and made sure that the fountain pen in the stand was filled. She put a clean blotter close by and then went into the other room. With the key to the Nurse's Station, Señora had given her the key to the small dispensary. Cherry checked the supplies while she sterilized various kinds of instruments which the doctor might need.

In the dispensary there were not only drugs for the asthmatics, but medication for cuts, bruises, sore throats, colds, and even a supply of morphine. There were also snake-bite kits, tourniquets, oxygen masks, and tanks containing a mixture of helium and oxygen. And there was a generous supply of everything which a doctor generally carries in his black bag. Among them were thermometers, tongue depressors, swabs, bandages, gauze, adhesive tape, scissors, tweezers, and a kit of scalpels.

Humming happily, Cherry shut off the sterilizer. In spite of Torry's dire predictions, she was enjoying her job. It was true that Mrs. Blair was a difficult, time-consuming patient, but Cherry felt that she understood her better now. It must be very hard for a woman who had once been a great beauty to accept an illness which was not only frightening—and consequently disfiguring because of the wrinkles which followed in the wake of pain and terror—but which was apparently incurable in Mrs. Blair's case.

"If I can just keep on feeling sorry for her instead of getting mad," Cherry decided, "we'll get along."

The letter to Harold Bean which Mrs. Blair had opened by mistake must have been written by Mr. Fleming, and if the latter finally bought the land, Harold Bean would go from rags to riches overnight. It was odd, though, that the Conrads, who had been such good friends of his father, apparently knew nothing about that valuable piece of property. Perhaps Patty's father had left her an equally valuable piece of property! If so, the deed to it might be in a secret place in The Castle, and the clues to where it was hidden somewhere between the lines of that enigmatic letter.

"I hope Jackie returns the key before Sunday," Cherry thought as she stood in front of the long mirror for a moment to make sure that she was still crisply immaculate in her head-to-toe white. She straightened her perky cap, then grinned ruefully.

"Be honest, Cherry," she said to her reflection, "before you meet Kirk Monroe again, you'd like to indulge in just a tiny bit of lipstick and powder. But that can't be and you ought to be thankful that at least you don't need rouge."

Then there was a tap on the door and she whirled guiltily away from the mirror as the tall, gray-eyed young doctor strode into the room. He was just as handsome and tanned as he had been when he had taken her dining and dancing in New York.

"Cherry!" he cried, holding out both hands. "You're prettier than ever. Gosh, it's great to be on duty with you again."

"It's great to be with you again, Kirk," she said. "I hope we'll get along as well as we did on the *Julita*."

"Of course we will," he said enthusiastically. "You and I are the greatest nurse-doctor team in the world." He took off his suit jacket and slipped on his white coat. "I want very much to catch up on everything that you've been doing since we last met, but I guess this morning the patients must come first. Any excitement?"

"No," Cherry said. "Mrs. Blair didn't feel up to having breakfast in the dining room, but everyone else is fine. So far as their T.P.R.'s are concerned, anyway. Jacqueline Longman lost her temper last evening at dinner. She was on the verge of crying with rage which worried me because I know that the mucus caused by crying can bring on an attack."

Kirk shrugged. "Those two, and Johnny Longman to a lesser degree, are the troublemakers around here. Mrs.

Blair really ought to have specials the minute she takes to her bed, but private duty nurses are as scarce as hen's teeth out here at this time of the year. And I don't like to waste 'em on hypochondriacs like Mrs. Blair. What we really need on this staff is a brisk young nurse's aide. Patty Doake would be perfect if she were only old enough to take the course. She could pass the exams with flying colors right now."

"She's a darling," Cherry said, as he scrubbed at the sink. "I suppose you know she wants to become a nurse."

He nodded. "I don't understand why her father didn't arrange things so that she would have at least enough money to carry her through training. He was a very rich man, but gambled away every cent on Wall Street. Poor Patty! She's too proud to accept charity from the Conrads. She's really silly to feel that way about those good people. They love her as much as though she were their own daughter and want more than anything else in the world to adopt her."

Using forceps, he took from the sterilizer some instruments and placed them in the sterile towel Cherry held out for him. Then they started off on the rounds.

"It's almost as good as being back on the wards at Spencer," Cherry thought with a little thrill. She had loved all of her various assignments, but working in a hospital, side by side with doctors, was the most satisfying kind of work of all.

CHAPTER VI

A Puzzling Conversation

AFTER THEY MADE THE ROUNDS, CHERRY AND KIRK RE-
turned to the Nurse's Station. As he made entries in the
Doctor's Order Book, he said:

"I think we might give Richie and Davie some sup-
plementary vitamins. They're shooting up like bean-
stalks. Nancy ought to cut down on sweets. She's getting
fat. If there were any sure way of keeping her from
eating between meals I'd let her have cake and pie for
dessert. But that girl will nibble constantly. So from
now on it's fruit or gelatin for dessert. She won't like
it, Cherry, when you enforce this order, but she's a good
kid, so you won't have any trouble."

"Perhaps," Cherry said thoughtfully, "I can persuade
Nancy to nibble on raw carrots and apples between
meals."

"A good idea," Kirk said. "Now, Mrs. Blair has been taking suppositories of aminophylline every four hours whenever she suffers from shortness of breath. I'm going to change that to intravenous injections of five hundred milligrams of aminophylline. Remember that it must be given very slowly. Allow about ten minutes for the injection." He shrugged. "It may help, but of course nothing really works with such an un-co-operative patient who makes no effort at self-control."

Cherry chuckled. "I was really surprised when we visited her that she didn't tell you to fire me. She said she was going to earlier this morning."

"What she says and what she does," Kirk told Cherry, "are two very different things. She knows very well that she'd be wasting her valuable breath if she told me to fire you."

He grinned at her, his gray eyes full of admiration. "Even if you weren't an excellent nurse I wouldn't fire you, Cherry Ames. Working with you makes business a pleasure. Beauty and brains is a rare combination."

Cherry laughed. "Mrs. Blair has somehow got the impression that I came out here for the sole purpose of getting a husband. Did you, by any chance, give her that impression?"

"That woman's a dangerous idiot," he exploded. "She suspects everyone of having ulterior motives. She's convinced that Mr. Neap wants to marry Mrs. Taper for her money, and that Mrs. Bloch has set her cap for rich Mr. Caudle. Whereas the truth of the matter is that those four are simply good friends who enjoy taking walks together and playing bridge in the evening and all that sort of thing. But just because the two women are widows and the two men are bachelors, Mrs. Blair is determined that their friendship will end in a double wedding."

"They're all wonderful patients," Cherry said. "I can't imagine any of them ever causing any trouble."

"They're very co-operative," Kirk agreed. "And not once since they've been spending their winters here in Tuscon have they ever had a severe attack." He changed his white coat for his tweed jacket. "I want to take you to dinner soon, Cherry, and show you the sights. Can you arrange things with Señora so you can have an evening off this week?"

"I don't think I should," Cherry said. "Not my first week here. I don't think Señora would like it. She thinks it's important that I get oriented and adjusted as fast as I can. I agree with her, but it will take at least a week, Kirk."

"Nonsense," he said. "You'll know the ropes perfectly by tomorrow evening. Old Pueblo, which is Tucson's nickname, is a fascinating city. We'll visit Old Town, the Mexican quarter, and the curio shops, and have dinner at the glamorous Pioneer. Then we'll drive out to the foothills and visit the San Xavier Mission, and come back to the Wishing Shrine, and end up with supper on the Santa Rita roof. It's a date, Cherry. Doctor's orders."

He left before she had a chance to argue. Cherry put the Nurse's Station to rights; then, locking the door behind her, returned to her own cubbyhole to freshen up before lunch. She put the key ring in her top bureau drawer, washed her face, and brushed her hair until it shone.

"Your face is shiny, too," she told her reflection in the mirror. "But it can't be helped. Mrs. Blair would be sure to send for you the moment you put on lipstick and powder."

When Cherry went out into the living room she joined the teen-agers who, with Harold Bean, were having tomato juice cocktails in front of one of the fireplaces. To Cherry's surprise, John and Jacqueline glanced at her coolly, turned their backs, and walked out to the patio.

Cherry stared after them, hurt and bewildered. They had been cordial and pleasant at breakfast. It was true that they had not spoken to her directly when she assisted the doctor during his checkup on them, but they had not been rude. They were being deliberately rude now. Why?

"Ames," Harold Bean was saying in his nasal voice,

"for I shall call you Ames, henceforth. Ames, I wish to have a word with you. Alone."

Nancy, Richie, and Davie promptly left to join the twins on the patio. Cherry bit her lip. Nurses, in a spirit of camaraderie, often called one another by their last names. But Harold Bean was not a nurse, nor was he a comrade, in the friend and companion sense of the word. She sensed that he looked down on her from his lofty intellectual heights and called her Ames in order to make sure that she kept her place.

Cherry was proud of her profession and resented anyone who did not respect it. She squared her shoulders and said with cold dignity: "Mr. Bean, I prefer that you call me Miss Ames. Especially when we are with the boys and girls. If I am to assist you in disciplining them, it is important that they respect me." Even in that moment when she was hot with resentment, Cherry couldn't help laughing at herself. She was beginning to talk exactly like this pompous tutor.

"Ames," he said, "your preferences in the matter do not make an iota of difference to me. I have always called the nurses by their last names, and I shall continue to do so. As for your gaining the respect of the boys and girls, you have lost your opportunity for that. If you had even a smattering of psychology, you would know that adolescents cannot condone falsehoods which are uttered by adults."

"I don't know what you're talking about," Cherry blurted. "If you don't start making some sense I shall refuse to continue this conversation."

He shrugged his bony shoulders. "Is it my fault that you are not capable of understanding the language of an educated person? However, henceforth, in your presence, I shall try to eliminate from my vocabulary words which apparently are beyond your comprehension. To be brief, the time has come for us to discuss our relative positions here at the hacienda. For they are related in that the Conrads, our employers, require the presence of one or both of us at all times in order to curb, shall we say, the high spirits of the younger generation. When I accepted the position of tutor here, I understood this fully. However, it was strictly understood at the time that I would receive the full co-operation of the resident nurse." He placed his almost fleshless finger tips together and rocked back and forth on his heels.

He looked so much like a giant scarecrow waving in the breeze that swept over the Illinois cornfields at pumpkin time that Cherry had a hard time suppressing her mirth. "I plan to co-operate fully, Mr. Bean," she said. "If you are worried for fear I may want to take an evening off at the same time that you may wish to do some research at the University, please put your mind at rest. Except for my weekly twenty-four hours off duty, I shall probably leave the ranch very seldom."

His pale eyebrows shot up above his horn-rimmed spectacles. "You surprise and amaze me, Ames. I hardly expected such a stay-at-home attitude from one who has such unusual pulchritude. What I mean to say is that you are both pretty and young." He folded his long, lean body into a deep but awkward bow. "Can you blame me for assuming that you would naturally wish to spend your evenings at the various Tucson night clubs?"

Cherry laughed. "Thanks for the compliment, if you meant it that way. No, Mr. Bean, I'm one of those people who require a lot of sleep. I couldn't possibly stay up late nights and do a good job the next day."

He held out one hand, with a smile that was intended to be gracious, turning up the corners of his lips. "You may call me Harold, Ames. I feel that we are going to be friends."

Cherry shook his hand. "I see no reason why we shouldn't be friends. I admire your ambition. A lot of young men wouldn't work so hard for a Ph.D."

The expression on his face became bitter. "It is especially hard for me, Ames, because I was, you might say, born with a silver spoon in my mouth. I always had more money than I could possibly spend until my father died suddenly in my junior year at the University. His lawyer could get together scarcely enough money to provide me with funds until, after graduation, I completed my academic requirements for my Ph.D. I am now working on my thesis: *How Early Indian Legends Compare with Legends of Other Primitive Tribes.* The theme is, as you can well imagine, one to which I should devote all of my time and energy. But, through no fault of my own, I am a pauper. The person to blame for my unfortunate predicament is—I should say, was—Patricia Doake's father."

Cherry's mouth fell open with surprise. "Why, what are you saying, Harold Bean? Patty's father died without leaving her a cent last summer. I understand that your father died almost three years ago."

"True," the tutor said, pursing his lips. "But when the two men came back from South America five years ago they were both extraordinarily wealthy. My father promised me then that I would never want for anything as long as I lived. To use his own words, he informed me that he had brought me back a nest egg. Where is that nest egg, Ames?"

"I have no idea," Cherry replied, although she knew the question was purely rhetorical.

"The answer is simple," he continued. "Some sort of a swindle took place, and Father was the victim."

"I don't believe it," Cherry said tartly. "Have you any proof?"

"Alas, no," he admitted. "That is to say, nothing which would have enabled me to take legal steps at the time of Father's demise. However, that is all water over

the dam. I have no hard feelings. Patricia is, to be col-
loquial, in the same boat with me. She has my sympathy.
But I can never forgive her father. His insatiable thirst
for gambling brought about our ruin."

The expression on his face and the bitter tone of his
voice told Cherry plainly that Harold Bean *did* have
hard feelings and that he had no sympathy at all for
Patty.

"However," he continued, "you are, of course, en-
titled to your own opinion. No one here has been able
to avoid noticing that you and Patricia have formed an
attachment for each other. She has what is commonly
known as a crush on you. You will, naturally, not wish
to believe that the girl's father was a professional criminal. However, for your own good, I must warn you."

"If he says 'however' one more time," Cherry thought,
"I'll scream."

"Señora," he added in a low voice, "does not approve
of crushes. If you wish to have your employers view you
with favor, you will, to make a pun, speedily crush said
crush."

Cherry couldn't help laughing. "I don't think Patty
has a crush on me," she said cheerfully. "Why, I hardly
see her. When she isn't having classes she's working."

"Moreover," he went on, just as though Cherry hadn't
made a remark, "you should also be made aware of the
fact that Señora, although a woman of high character,

will do everything she can to take advantage of you. There is, for instance, no real reason why you should have anything whatsoever to do with the disciplining of the youngsters. You are a registered nurse, not a governess. But during those hours when you, as a nurse, would normally be free to do as you please, you will find that you are serving in the capacity of a governess. Take my advice. Refuse flatly from the onset to do anything more than you have previously agreed to do. Stand up for your rights, Ames. A word to the wise," he finished with a sly wink, "is sufficient."

The luncheon gong sounded then and he hurried off. Cherry followed him slowly into the dining room. The tutor, she decided, was far too complex a character for her ever to understand. He seemed to be very bitter because his father had not left him a nest egg, and yet he was obviously the owner of a valuable piece of property which he was selling to Mr. Fleming.

And, for a few minutes during their conversation, she had thought that he really wanted to be her friend. But now she wasn't so sure. If she followed his advice, although it may have been well meant, Cherry knew perfectly well that she wouldn't be popular with anyone, least of all with Señora.

CHAPTER VII

The Missing Key Ring

LUNCH WAS A DISMAL MEAL FOR CHERRY. THE TWINS talked constantly to everyone else at the table, completely ignoring her presence. If they had been as rude to anyone but herself, Cherry would have scolded them, but since she was the victim she knew that anything she said would be interpreted as a personal rebuke.

Patty struggled vainly to bring Cherry into the conversation, but the voices of the others drowned her out. Several times their voices were so loud and shrill that Cherry felt it necessary to "Sh-h" them, and whenever they talked with their mouths full she frowned and shook her head to register her disapproval. Supervising their table manners was part of her job, and all of a sudden Cherry realized that she was, in a way, performing the duty of a governess. And it was neither easy nor pleasant. She was too young herself to fall naturally into the role of a strict martinet, and since their attitude was far from friendly, everything she said or did only increased their hostility.

Another part of her job as both nurse and governess was to see to it that they rested for an hour after lunch. The boys and girls were fully aware of this rule and she hoped fervently that there would be no necessity for her to enforce it. But she hoped in vain.

The twins bolted their dessert, mumbled "May I be excused," pushed back their chairs, and said to the others, "Come on. Let's play ping-pong."

Cherry glanced at Harold Bean. Surely he would say something. If he really wanted to be her friend he must realize that this was her first day on duty and so would do everything possible to help her. To her dismay, he didn't even glance up, concentrating as usual on transferring food from his plate to his mouth, as though the world would come to an end if he didn't get his full quota of calories, minerals, and vitamins.

Cherry pushed back her own chair and stood up. She moved swiftly to the double doors, turned, and stood there, blocking the way to the patio. "You boys and girls are to go to your rooms at once," she said crisply. "And you are to rest quietly for the next hour. I'll give you ten minutes and then I'm going to check up on you. Do you understand?"

Jacqueline's black eyes flashed. "Don't talk to me in that tone of voice, *nurse*," she said disdainfully. "I'll do just as I please, and if you try to interfere, I'll report you to *Mrs.* Conrad."

Cherry chose her own words carefully. "Jackie, you know as well as I do that I will only be following both the doctor's and Señora's orders when I enforce this rule. It's a good rule, Jackie, and you know that it is."

"Pooh," Jacqueline said defiantly. "You couldn't make me do anything. And I wasn't going to report you to Mrs. Conrad for that. I was going to tell her that you are a . . ."

The rest of her words were lost in the din and confusion which was caused by the fact that the older guests were leaving their tables now, talking across the room to one another as they started toward the patio. Cherry was forced to move away from the entrance, and in a minute the teen-agers were lost in the crowd on the patio.

"Never mind," Patty whispered close to her ear. "They're not really going to play ping-pong, Cherry. Jackie just said that to tease. I have to help clear the tables now, but as soon as I finish drying the silver, I'll come to your room and explain everything."

Harold Bean, the last person in the room to finish eating, patted his mouth with his napkin, meticulously folded it, and pushed back his chair. Patty and the waitresses were working in the far end of the huge room, so he and Cherry were alone by the double glass doors.

"Ames," he said as he moved awkwardly toward her, "you need more of my expert advice. If you value your position here, do not, under any circumstances, cross the Longman twins in any way. Jacqueline has a violent temper. The slightest clash of wills inevitably brings on an attack. If she has frequent attacks, her father, who, I may as well add for your further information is a very wealthy man, will remove her and her brother to another ranch. To be crass and a bit vulgar, the Longman twins and Mrs. Blair are the Conrads' bread and butter. They pay three times as much for their suites as Neap, Taper, Bloch, and Caudle do for their single rooms. Moreover, unlike the transient occupants of the cabins, the Longman twins and Mrs. Blair arrive in September and stay until the end of May. If you multiply the sum total of their monthly statements by eight, representing the number of months they remain here as paying guests, you will arrive at the stupendous figure of approximately sixty-five hundred dollars."

Cherry stared at him blankly. "I don't understand what all this business about money has to do with me."

He waved a bony finger under her nose. "Ah, but you will; in fact, you must, for on your comprehension of it, depends your own bread and butter. If you do not get along well with the star boarders; viz., Blair, Longman, and Longman, you are, to put it bluntly, fired."

"Oh, don't be silly," Cherry said crossly. "That's not the point. Naturally, no one likes to be dismissed. But so far as my bread and butter is concerned, it does not depend on this job. You may not know it, but there is a terrific shortage of nurses all over the world. I didn't come here because I was unemployed. I came here because I wanted to. If Señora finds me unsatisfactory, I'll resign. In my own home town alone there are three jobs waiting for me: in the Hilton Hospital, the clinic, and in the new nursing home. I'm not boasting," she finished, "but I do think it's high time some of the people around here had more respect for my profession."

He elevated his pale eyebrows. "You may or may not know it, but there is also a dearth of educated, intellectual, well-bred, competent tutors, Ames. By merely picking up the phone, I could command a far, far higher salary than I am receiving here."

"I'm sure you could," Cherry said blandly. "Why don't you?"

He drew himself up to his full height, and if the ceilings hadn't been so high, he would have bumped his head. "That," he said grandly, "is no concern of yours."

"You're absolutely right," Cherry heartily agreed. "Nor is it any concern of yours how I conduct myself here as a nurse. Right now, I'm going to make sure that every one of the teen-agers, including the Longman twins, is resting. As a nurse, I happen to know that it is important for their health that they do." She gave him a shrewd, calculating glance. "I'm going to count on your co-operation, because I understand that you share in this responsibility. Will you come with me, or shall I send for you if I need you?"

He folded up like an accordion and sank into the nearest chair. "My dear Ames," he finally got out in a squeaky voice, "you apparently have not grasped the situation fully. If I should assist you in forcing the Longman twins into obeying the rules and regulations, and thus be party to causing one or both of them to have an attack, I would be asked to resign."

"So what?" Cherry cried exasperatedly. "To use your own words, you can command a far higher salary elsewhere by simply picking up the phone. Surely you can't enjoy your job here since you admit yourself that you are forced to kowtow to the star boarders. In my profession we are taught as probationers that there is no distinction between rich and poor. I was under the impression that the same rule applied in the field of education."

He said nothing, his skeletal face expressionless, but Cherry sensed that he was inwardly seething. She shrugged. It was all too, too baffling. Harold Bean, for reasons of his own which mystified her, was obviously not going to do anything which might jeopardize his position at the hacienda. That meant she could not count on his co-operation when it came to disciplining the twins. So there was only one course to take: she would carry on alone as best she could.

She glanced at her wrist watch. Ten minutes had elapsed since the boys and girls had left the dining room. They might be in the cabin where the ping-pong tables were, but on the other hand, they might be in their rooms. She decided to give them the benefit of doubt, because Patty had hinted that the twins were only teasing her.

Cherry checked up first on Richie and Davie. They were stretched out on top of their beds reading comics. Except for a bored "Come in" when she knocked, they ignored her. Cherry went on to Nancy's room. The plump girl was propped up in bed, reading a comic magazine. Beside her was a big valentine box of chocolate candy. As Cherry poked her head around the door, Nancy carefully selected a large piece and popped it into her mouth.

Cherry hesitated only a second, then she marched over to the bed. "All right, Nancy," she said gently. "I respect you for not hiding that box from me, but I'm going to ask you to give it to me. The doctor's orders are that you must cut out sweets. Both at meals and between meals."

"I don't care," Nancy said stormily. "I'm hungry."

Cherry smiled. "But you wouldn't be hungry if you had eaten all of your lunch. You were so busy talking you didn't touch your vegetables or salad or your delicious dessert of spiced pears."

Nancy turned her face to the wall. "It's not fair. Everybody else had potatoes and ice cream and cake. Even Patty who's just a poor little orphan. If they're going to starve me here, my father and mother will take me away."

Cherry sighed. "It isn't a question of starving you, Nancy. It's a question of your health *and* your happiness. It's not true that all fat people are healthy and jolly. Often they are sick people and miserable because they can't lose weight. Nobody wants you to lose weight. We just don't want you to gain too much too fast."

Suddenly Nancy burst into tears. "I *am* too fat. Jackie never stops making fun of me. But when she hurts my feelings I eat a piece of candy and then I don't seem to mind so much."

Cherry nodded sympathetically. "At times like that, why don't you try eating a big red apple or some nice crisp, salty celery and carrot strips?" She touched her fingers to Nancy's pulse, watching her respiration. Cherry had not anticipated tears when she had decided to help Nancy curb her appetite. Tears which might result in an attack. "Stop crying, Nancy," she said soothingly. "You're not too fat. When you grow a couple of more inches you'll be as slim as a cricket."

Instantly Nancy turned around to face Cherry. "Is

that true, Miss Ames? I mean, I won't be fat all of my life, will I?"

"Of course not," Cherry said. "Why don't you let me bring you something good to eat right now that isn't fattening? You can nibble on celery and carrots and an apple while you rest and read. Then you won't be hungry again until dinnertime. As soon as you stop eating candy between meals, Dr. Monroe will let you have pie and cake and ice cream for dessert again."

Nancy's round face was wreathed in smiles. "You make it sound easy, Miss Ames. You're nice. Patty said you were just darling. But Jackie said—said—well, never mind. I don't believe her. And I would like something to nibble on now, if it isn't too much trouble. And could I call you Cherry? Patty does."

"Of course," Cherry said. "I love to be called by my nickname. And I tell you what I think you ought to do. Instead of giving that beautiful box of candy to me, why don't you give it to Mrs. Bloch or Mrs. Taper? They could serve it in those tiny Mexican silver bonbon dishes during their evening bridge games."

Nancy nodded. "I'd like to do that."

Cherry left then and went on to the twins' suite. She knocked. No answer. She knocked again and opened the door. Jacqueline and Johnny were seated cross-legged on the beautiful Navaho rug with a deck of cards fanned out between them. As she came into the room they each picked up a card and gazed at it intently. The expression on their faces made Cherry feel sure that they had been up to something very, very recently.

Jacqueline was in a defiant mood, but Johnny looked as though he were suffering from a guilty conscience. He glanced up at her out of the corner of one black eye and said sheepishly:

"Oh, hello."

"Hello," Cherry returned. "Is this the way you two usually rest?"

The boy scrambled to his feet. "Well, not exactly. Guess I'll go to my own room now. Feel kinda tired."

"I think you'd better lie down, too," Cherry said to Jacqueline. "I'll help you pick up the cards."

"Don't bother," Jacqueline cried rudely. "Go away, *please!* And don't worry. I'll go to bed. But not because you told me to."

Cherry stooped and began to form the scattered cards into a pack. "Jacqueline," she said quietly, "I don't know what I've done or said to make you dislike me. I wish you'd tell me."

Jacqueline leaped to her feet. "If you don't go away I'll scream."

"Very well." Cherry placed the deck of cards on the bedside table and walked slowly out to the living room. She went straight to the kitchen where Patty introduced her to the jolly, pleasant-faced Mexican cook.

As Patty helped Cherry fix a plate for Nancy she said, "I'll be through here in a few minutes. See you in your room."

"Fine," Cherry said. She pushed her way through the swinging doors into the dining room. Señora was seated at one of the tables, making corrections on the menus. She looked up and stared at Cherry in amazement.

"My goodness, Cherry," she cried, "what have you there? Are you keeping a pet rabbit in your room?"

Cherry laughed and explained. "I hope I haven't broken any rules," she finished.

"Heavens, no," Señora said with a chuckle. "But you are not a maid, Cherry Ames. If Nancy wanted a snack, all she had to do was ring her little brass dinner bell."

"I know," Cherry admitted. "But I think she needs encouragement right now."

Señora laughed. "I see your point. If Nancy had had the choosing, the snack would have consisted of chocolate ice cream with butterscotch sauce. But I don't want any of our guests to take advantage of you, Cherry. Asthmatics, as you know, are apt to be selfish and demanding. We have to humor them all, but if any one of them, including Mrs. Blair, tries to make a slave girl of you, let me know at once."

So, Cherry thought, as she hurried on to Nancy's room, this is the woman Harold Bean assured me would do everything she could to take advantage of me! After she left Nancy she decided that this would be a good time to attach to the adult patients' charts the sheets from the Doctor's Order Book. It would take but a few minutes and at the same time she could ask each one if he or she wanted anything to make them comfortable.

Back in her little cell, Cherry opened her top bureau drawer. Then she let out a gasp of surprise. The key ring she had placed there before lunch was gone!

~~~~~~

CHAPTER VIII

More Trouble

ALTHOUGH THE DRAWER WAS QUITE LARGE, IT CONtained nothing but Cherry's stockings and handkerchiefs, so it took only a minute for her to make absolutely sure that the key ring was missing. On it was the key to the dispensary, and in that cupboard were all sorts of drugs which would be lethally dangerous in the hands of a layman!

Just then Patty came in. "Why, Cherry, what on earth is the matter? You look as though you'd seen a ghost!"

Cherry hastily explained. "I know I put them right here," she finished. "Señora couldn't have taken them (a) because she wouldn't have known where I put them, and (b) because she has a set of her own. Who could have taken them, Patty?"

"The twins," Patty said promptly. "So don't worry, Cherry. They'll bring back the Nurse's Station key ring."

"I can't wait until they get around to returning it," Cherry said. "Suppose they decided to raid the dispensary? Adrenalin—"

"They wouldn't do that," Patty said soothingly. "They're not really bad kids, Cherry. They just took the keys to annoy you." She frowned suddenly. "No, they probably took them to get you into trouble. In that case they would have left them in the door of the station where Señora would see them and think that you were careless. I'll go see." She darted off and came right back with the key ring in her hand. "There! I'm a pretty good detective myself, aren't I?"

"You certainly are." Cherry let out a sigh of relief. "But why do they want to get me into trouble, Patty?"

"Because they don't think you're really and truly a twin, Cherry." Patty curled up in the chair as Cherry stretched out wearily on the bed. "While we were having a study period this morning, I heard them whispering about you to the others. Nancy and Richie and Davie, you know. They didn't dare say anything to me. I tried not to listen at first, but I couldn't help hearing snatches. They think you fibbed about being a twin to get on the good side of them."

"I don't understand," Cherry moaned. "Last evening

they believed me. And this morning at breakfast they did. What changed them, Patty?"

"I don't know." Patty shook her head. "And I can't find out, because they're not speaking to me. They did go to the ping-pong cabin after lunch. I saw them through the window and went out through the kitchen door and I told them that if they didn't go straight to their rooms I'd tell Señora. I'm not a tattletale, but I'm not going to let them get you into trouble."

"You're sweet, Patty," Cherry said gratefully. "But you mustn't try to fight my battles for me. I could easily prove to them that I am a twin if only Charlie and I looked more alike. Oh," she interrupted herself. "That explains it. I told Jackie last evening that she could come into my room any time she liked and see Charlie's picture."

"That did it all right," Patty said with a rueful chuckle. "He doesn't look much more like you than Harold Bean does. I mean, Charlie is so tall and broad-shouldered and blond!"

"I *could* ask Dr. Joe for our birth certificates," Cherry said with an equally rueful chuckle. "But I won't. Anyway, from now on I'm going to carry the keys around with me whenever I leave the room. Or, better still, think up some good hiding place for them."

"I know a good place," Patty said. "The toe of one of your riding boots."

"Why is that a good place?" Cherry demanded. "It'll only mean that I'll have to take the keys with me when I go riding. Suppose I dropped the ring out on the desert?"

Patty giggled. "No, it won't, because you're never going to wear those boots, Cherry. They're English boots and nobody out here wears anything but cowboy boots. I've got an extra pair of the right kind with high heels. They're very prettily decorated, too. You'll like them, Cherry, and I'm sure they'll fit. You wear a 5 A, too, don't you?"

Cherry nodded. "But I can't borrow all of your things, Patty. It's my own fault for coming out here with all the wrong things."

"Oh, everyone does the first time," Patty assured her. "The reason for high-heeled boots is that they keep your foot from slipping clear through the stirrup. That's important if you should ever get thrown and the horse runs away. You'd get dragged and badly hurt if your foot was caught in the stirrup. Cowboys like high heels for another reason, too. They dig them into the ground when they're roping a horse or steer on foot. My boots are the kind with short uppers which are worn by rodeo riders to brace their ankles when they fall. Anyway, Cherry, I want you to borrow them, and also I wish you'd let me hide my key and letter in the toe of one of your English boots. It's a good safe place, and now that the twins are mad at me, Jackie might take that brown envelope again just when we planned to search The Castle for clues."

"*Again?*" Cherry repeated in amazement. "Do you mean to stand there, Patty Doake, and tell me that the key and the letter have been returned?"

"That's right," Patty said with a smile. "I found the envelope a few minutes ago in my night-table drawer. Jackie must have put it back some time before lunch. She was in and out of the classroom all morning."

"Why, what do you mean?" Cherry asked. "She was only called away from her classes once—when the doctor sent for her."

Patty shook her head. "We didn't have any classes this morning. Harold told us what to study, then he drove off somewhere. He didn't get back until just before lunch. He's been doing that a lot lately."

"Surely not with the Conrads' permission?" Cherry asked incredulously.

"Oh, no," Patty replied. "They're so busy in the morning that it's easy for him to sneak out and back without being seen. And none of us would ever tattle."

"No wonder he works here for such a small salary," Cherry said impatiently. "The answer is that he's not working for the Conrads; he spends most of his time getting material for his thesis."

Patty shrugged. "Even if Señora and Uncle Frank knew that he really doesn't do much more than give us assignments and tests and correct our papers, they wouldn't fire him. They feel sorry for him because Harold's father didn't leave him enough money so he could get his Ph.D. without having to take a job."

"That's ridiculous," Cherry exploded. "Harold Bean doesn't need charity. He owns some very valuable property." Too late she clapped her hand over her mouth. "Oh, I shouldn't have said that, Patty."

Patty stared at her. "Why *did* you say it? Harold's father didn't leave him any land except half of that acre on which The Castle was built. When Mr. Bean died, Daddy sent Harold a big check and Harold signed a paper giving Daddy all rights to the property. Mr. Dawson had a new deed drawn up then, naming Daddy as sole owner. I saw the deed, Cherry."

"But," Cherry argued, "Mr. Bean may have left Harold some other property. Maybe a mine in Alaska."

"I wouldn't know about that," Patty admitted. "But Mr. Dawson would. He was Mr. Bean's lawyer, too, and he told me that the only thing Harold inherited was that half share of The Castle. And that wasn't worth a tenth of what Daddy paid Harold."

"H-m-m," Cherry mumbled thoughtfully. "So Mr. Dawson was old Mr. Bean's lawyer. Has he been out of town a lot recently, Patty?"

"Why, no," Patty replied. "He's been coming out here or talking to me on the phone about once a week.

He's so bound and determined that I should become the Conrads' adopted daughter that he's even drawn up the papers. So far as I know he hasn't left town for months."

Cherry suddenly made up her mind. She told Patty then about the conversation she had overheard in the airport terminal. "I think we ought to report it to Mr. Dawson," she finished. "Harold Bean is obviously trying to sell property on which there is valuable ore. It could be the land around The Castle and he may feel for some reason that he still owns part of it."

Patty laughed. "All I own is an acre of desert, Cherry. The foothills belong to the Conrads. Harold must have inherited some property which Mr. Dawson didn't know about."

"I guess that's the answer," Cherry reluctantly agreed. "I was hoping your nest egg might turn out to be a gold mine."

Patty got the brown envelope from her room and gave Cherry the original of her father's letter. "Please read it again," she begged. "I might have left out an important clue."

But, except for the fact that the handwriting was the spidery scrawl which had been fashionable in a bygone era, the two letters were identical. "It may be packed with clues," Cherry said cheerfully, "but until I've seen The Castle I won't be able to recognize them."

Patty tucked the brown envelope into one of Cherry's

boots. "Why couldn't we search this afternoon?" she asked wistfully. "Nobody's sick, so there isn't any reason why you and I and Torry couldn't ride out to The Castle. The others won't want to go because of swimming lessons at the pool. And Torry does want to go. He told me so this morning, Cherry. He thinks you're just wonderful."

"He's very attractive," Cherry said with a blush. "I'm glad he likes me because I like him. It would be fun to go for a ride with you two, if Señora approves."

Señora did approve. "But," she said to Cherry, "it's a wild-goose chase. I know you have a reputation as a detective, and Patty's counting on you to help her find that missing nest egg. I don't want to discourage either of you, but there just isn't one. Not any more. Both Patty's and Harold's fathers amassed large fortunes several times, but inevitably they lost everything through wild speculations. However, run along and have fun." Her dark eyes twinkled. "And as for tomorrow evening, that's all right, too. Dr. Monroe called me a few minutes ago to say that he wanted to take you sight-seeing."

Cherry's cheeks flamed again. "I told him that I didn't want to go, Señora. Not this first week. It's very inconvenient for both you and Mr. Bean. Both of you have to stay here if I go out. Frankly, I'd rather not go out in the evening at all, except perhaps on my regular day off."

Señora waved her slim hands expressively. "But you

must keep your date with the handsome young doctor, my dear. It has all been arranged. I myself have no desire to leave the hacienda any evening this week. And as you must know by now, Harold Bean is a very co-operative young man. When I asked him if he could adjust his schedule so you can leave tomorrow afternoon around five, he said he was more than willing to do so."

"Thank you, Señora," Cherry said, and left the office thinking: "Señora really couldn't be nicer, and Harold Bean seems to be co-operative after all. Maybe all of my worries are due to the fact that I just haven't become adjusted yet to the personalities here."

She went on to the Nurse's Station then to get the sheets from the Doctor's Order Book so she could transfer them to each patient's chart. To her surprise and horror, Mrs. Blair's sheet was not in the loose-leaf notebook. It had been the very first one because Blair came first alphabetically. Cherry herself had written the names of the ten patients on each blank sheet in alphabetical order before the doctor arrived. And although Kirk had skipped around as he wrote his orders, he had not changed Cherry's arrangement. She was sure of that, and in a few minutes, after skimming every page in the big book, she had to face the fact that Mrs. Blair's sheet was missing.

This was too much. The twins had obviously taken it in order to get her into trouble. But since she had absolutely no way of proving that it was they who had taken the key ring in the first place, her hands were tied.

"Oh, dear," Cherry moaned. "Mrs. Blair may have a mild attack any minute. In that case she should have an intravenous injection of aminophylline. But I can't change the order on her chart because I haven't got the new sheet with the latest order."

It was a hopeless predicament for any resident nurse to find herself in, especially on her first day on duty. If she accused Jacqueline of taking the sheet, it might precipitate an attack, and she would get nowhere in the end. If she called Kirk Monroe, it would only make him lose confidence in her as a competent nurse because she could not possibly explain the whole situation to him over the phone. Besides, he was not in his office now and would certainly not like to be disturbed while he was making calls.

Cherry squared her shoulders. There was only one thing to do; go to Señora and confess.

CHAPTER IX

~~~~~~

The Mystery Castle

SEÑORA WAS STILL IN THE DINING ROOM WORKING ON
the menus. She finished correcting one, blotted it, and
slipped it back into its bright jacket. Then she looked up
and smiled at Cherry. "What can I do for you, my dear?"

Cherry gulped. She was staring at the jacket on top of
the pile which Señora had not yet corrected. It did not
contain a menu; it contained Mrs. Blair's missing sheet
from the Doctor's Order Book!

Señora followed her eyes to it, and it was her turn
to gulp. "Good heavens," she cried in amazement. "How
on earth did that get there?" Her eyes, flashing fire of
anger, traveled back to Cherry's crimson face. "Surely,
Miss Ames, this is not your idea of a joke?"

Weakly, wordlessly, Cherry sank into the chair opposite Señora. She must gather her scattered thoughts quickly. To tell Señora that she suspected the twins would come under the heading of being a tattletale, an unforgivable sin in the eyes of teen-agers. Furthermore, she had no proof that the twins *had* played this prank.

At last Cherry said forlornly, "I don't know who put the sheet in the menu jacket or why. Anyway, someone took the Nurse's Station key ring from my bureau drawer and left it in the lock. Before that, he or she or they must have taken this sheet from the Doctor's Order Book and put it here where you would be sure to find it."

Señora stared unseeingly through the picture window at the yellow and orange and purple mountains in the distance. At last she said, "Well, I must believe you, although nothing like this has ever happened before. Please see to it that the key ring is never again available to a practical joker. Take this sheet and attach it to Mrs. Blair's chart at once. I don't suppose I have to instruct you that you should then check the entire Nurse's Station to make sure that nothing else is missing."

Cherry nodded and fled, too close to tears to say a word. Just a few minutes ago Señora had been so kind and friendly, and now she was as cold as ice. Cherry transferred all the sheets to the patients' charts, and although she felt very down in the dumps, she managed to say a pleasant word or two to each one during the process. The members of the Foursome, as Cherry now thought of Mr. Neap, Mr. Caudle, Mrs. Taper, and Mrs. Bloch, thanked her for dropping in, but Mrs. Blair complained that Cherry had awakened her from a sound sleep.

"I'm sorry," Cherry said. "I'll put the Do Not Disturb sign on your door."

"If it isn't too much trouble," Mrs. Blair said sarcastically. "I do not wish to detain you. I happen to know that you are going for a ride this afternoon with the handsome young foreman. And that tomorrow night you are going out with the handsome young doctor. We guests must be sure that you are not tired and haggard. Although I should like my knees raised slightly, I should not think of asking you to do so."

Cherry adjusted the bed. "Is there anything else I can do for you, Mrs. Blair?"

The old woman moaned fretfully and turned her face to the wall. Cherry put the sign on the door and hurried back to the station. It took an hour to check everything thoroughly, and she was tired when she locked the door, but glad that nothing was out of order.

Cherry changed quickly from uniform to Levis and the bright checkered cowboy shirt Charlie had given her. She was slipping on wool socks when Patty arrived with the boots she insisted upon lending Cherry.

"Oh, they're beautiful," Cherry cried. "Hand-tooled uppers! Much too good for me."

"The ones I have on cost twice as much," Patty said. "But I like yours better, for you. I brought along boot hooks in case you didn't bring any. Out here we call bootstraps 'mule ears.'"

Cherry pulled on the boots and took a few toppling steps to the mirror. "Oh me, oh my," she moaned, "I can't even walk, let alone ride. I've been wearing sensible shoes for so long I've forgotten what high heels feel like."

Patty laughed. "It'll all come back to you quickly. Like riding a bike, you know. And it's only a few yards to the corral where Torry has our horses ready and to use the lingo, 'waiten fer us, ma'am.'"

Cherry giggled. "Please put the Nurse's Station key ring in the toe of my despicable boots, ma'am, if you'll be so kind. If I should attempt such a thing in my present condition, I'd fall on my face."

Shaking with laughter, Patty dove into the tiny closet and came back with the brown envelope. "Now we're all set," she said. "We have the key to The Castle and Daddy's letter, Cherry. Take my arm, ma'am. And stop teetering and tottering. The idea is to swagger!"

Cherry clutched Patty's arm, thrown off balance as much by suppressed laughter as she was by the high-heeled boots. By the time they reached the path that led from the patio entrance to the corral she had, as she told Patty gaily, "got her sea legs back."

Torry, looking more handsome than ever, met them at the corral gate, leading three saddled and bridled horses. His eyes twinkled as he helped Cherry mount a docile-looking strawberry roan. "Don't mention the sea to me, Cherry Ames. It reminds me of that cruise you went on with my rival, Dr. Monroe."

Not too awkwardly, but certainly not expertly, Cherry managed to settle into the saddle without, as she had feared, sailing over it to land on the other side. "The sea I was referring to," she said as Torry adjusted her stirrups, "was the desert. Not the Caribbean. I thought I'd seen Nature in her brightest colors on that cruise, but out here the colors seem much brighter. This morning, when I pulled the drapery cord on my window, the sunrise was so dazzling I felt blinded by its beauty."

"This is the only place to live," Torry said as he swung up into his saddle. "But you mustn't try to take it all in at once, Cherry. It's too big. When I first came out here as a kid I felt blinded, too. Now, take our ride out to The Castle. It's about twenty miles round trip. Maybe it's too much for you the first day."

Cherry shook her head. "I did twenty miles two days' running before I left home. Just to get in practice. I wasn't stiff or sore at all afterward."

"Good for you," he said approvingly. "Out here distances don't mean anything. It's almost seventy miles to Nogales on the Mexican border, but nobody thinks anything of going there for lunch. We'll have lunch there your first day off. Next Sunday. Won't we?"

"No, you won't," Patty said firmly. "Cherry's going to spend most of her first day off helping me look for my nest egg, aren't you, Cherry?"

"Maybe we'll find it today," Cherry said cheerfully. "Is it all right to canter now?"

"Sure," Torry said, "but watch out for gopher holes."

They loped along for about ten minutes, then Patty said, "You can see the tower room now." She pointed to a blob of gold that seemed to Cherry to be suspended in mid-air above the blue foothills. "Daddy used some special kind of gilt paint. I don't know why. But then, I don't really know why he built The Castle at all."

"It's a strange place, all right," Torry said. "That pie-shaped foundation gets me. Why three walls instead of four?"

"I can guess," Cherry said. "It doesn't take as long to erect three walls as it does four. And since the two men did all the work themselves, I imagine they took a lot of short cuts."

"I frankly don't know how they did it," Torry admitted. "That skylight in the tower room is the work of an expert. Your father and Mr. Bean," he said to Patty, "must have been Jacks-of-all-trades."

"I guess they were," Patty agreed. "I know they worked at all sorts of jobs when they were boys."

They were in the foothills now, and although very close to The Castle, all Cherry could see of it was the cupola. Then they swerved sharply to the south until the knoll which hid The Castle from view sloped away into nothing. As it sloped down into the desert, Cherry caught glimpses of the front of The Castle until at last they were there, just a few feet from the massive oak door.

Although Cherry had expected to see an odd-looking piece of architecture, she couldn't help gasping with surprise. Because of its shape, all she could see was the front wall, which formed the base of the triangle. The other two walls were not visible, so this part of The Castle looked as though it were simply a wall, standing there alone in the semicircle formed by the foothills.

The front wall was about eighteen feet high and windowless. But above it, beneath what Cherry guessed was a flat roof, was a solid row of huge plate-glass windows. She dismounted in silence, thinking that Mr. Doake must have been very eccentric indeed—*unless*, he had a reason for placing the windows so high that there would never be any danger of his being spied upon.

Torry led the horses to a shrubby mesquite and looped the reins around the branches in a half hitch. "Don't say a word until you've seen the interior." He grinned.

Patty unlocked the door and led the way inside. Cherry, consumed with curiosity, hurried after her. Now she could see that The Castle was, as Patty had said, nothing but one big room. A circular staircase wound its way up to a balcony with low wrought-iron railings. The outer wall of the balcony was formed by the big picture windows. And the tower room, with its skylight, had been built in the V of the triangle.

Cherry's high heels clacked on the tile floor as she trotted into the center of the room. The desk and book-case unit took up most of the space under the south bal-cony. Under the balcony on the north side were two big sofa beds. The largest had obviously been a four-poster at one time, but the posts had been sawed off.

"Bed," Cherry said aloud without realizing it. "It's the third word in your father's letter, Patty. 'Early to bed and early to rise.' I wonder if those posts are hollow."

Before she had finished speaking, Torry had dragged the divan out from under the floor of the balcony. "I'll be a monkey's uncle," he said. "These knobs on top of the posts look as though they had been screwed on. I thought they were all one solid piece of wood, didn't you, Patty?"

Patty didn't bother to reply. She quickly unscrewed the knob that was closest to her and reached her hand inside. "Hollow, all right," she said. "But empty."

"Same here," Cherry and Torry said simultaneously.

Patty darted around to the fourth and last post. Before anyone had time to say a word, she had removed the knob and taken from the interior a scrap of paper.

"Oh, oh," she cried, collapsing on the sofa bed. "It's in Daddy's handwriting. You read it, Cherry. I can't. I'm too excited."

Cherry was only too glad to take the scrap from Patty and read the message:

> " '*My darling daughter:*
> " '*Remember that I was always an early riser and that I started out as a poor man, working my way up to the top of the ladder, step by step.*' "

"Oh," Patty said disappointedly. "More good advice. I guess there's no doubt now that Daddy meant for me to work my way up to the top, too."

"Maybe there's something else inside this post," Cherry said. She reached down as far as she could, and when she drew out her hand, there was a little tobacco sack in it. "Feels like money," she told Patty. "Empty it on the bed."

Sure enough, it was filled with money: silver dollars, quarters, and dimes.

"Well, there's your nest egg," Torry said, and Cherry knew he was trying to sound cheerful. "It couldn't amount to more than fifteen dollars, but it shows your old man had good intentions, Patty. That tobaccy bag was probably filled with gold pieces once."

"I guess so," Patty said.

"I don't agree with you," Cherry said stanchly. "Your father had to have some money in cash to buy supplies with. And he kept it in this hollow post. It's just a coincidence that he put this note to you in the same place. But it's not a coincidence that we found it. The clue was right there in his letter. I'm sure there are other clues in that letter and at least one clue in this note."

Patty brightened. "I suppose we have to go back to the hacienda now, but you'll help me look again, Cherry?"

"Of course," Cherry told her. "As soon as I get off duty on Sunday we'll come out here and spend the whole day if necessary."

"That's a date," Torry said happily. "Instead of lunching in Mexico, we'll have a picnic here. We'll bring our grub in saddlebags and cook it on the barbecue pit outside where Mr. Doake probably did most of his cooking. And—"

"Oh, oh," Patty interrupted suddenly. "Somebody's been here since we were here last week, Torry."

"Impossible," he said firmly. "Nobody could get in without the key. That lock was made to order. No other key in this wide world would fit it."

"But look," Patty said, pointing. "The books in the

bookcase aren't the way we left them. When I put them back after you made sure that the shelves were built in, I put the large books on the bottom and the small ones on top. Now they're all helter-skelter."

Torry chuckled. "You *thought* you replaced them the way your father kept them, but you were in an awful hurry, remember? It's like Bill. When I tell him to police up the tack room, he starts out with good intentions but ends up with everything topsy-turvy."

"He sounds like my neighbor, Midge Fortune," Cherry said as they went outside. Patty locked the door, put the key back into the brown envelope, and handed it to Cherry.

They mounted their horses and cantered back toward the ranch house. "Tell me more about Midge," Patty said. "I'd love to meet her sometime. I'd like to meet all of your friends. They sound so interesting."

"Maybe you will," Cherry said. "I'm going to write an air-mail letter to Gwen and Josie this evening. I'm going to tell them that Tucson is the place where they should spend their vacation."

She related some of Midge's hilarious escapades then, but with another part of her mind she was thinking:

Patty is a very tidy person. She didn't put those books back helter-skelter. Somebody else did. Whoever took that envelope from her drawer Saturday night could have had a duplicate key made before returning it.

It might have been the twins, but they had no motive for searching The Castle nor any opportunity to do so. Who did have both motive and opportunity?

"Someone," she decided that night as she began her letter to Gwen and Josie, "who thinks as I do that something valuable is hidden in that strange architectural horror."

CHAPTER X

~~~~~~

An Unhappy Week

IT WAS SATURDAY NIGHT AND CHERRY SAT FORLORNLY alone in her little cell. It had been a miserable week. No letters from home, no letters from the gang, and her mother had not sent the box of evening frocks. Of course the package might have been delayed somewhere en route, but there was no explanation of why she hadn't received at least one air-mail letter from someone.

Cherry's mother always wrote two or three times a week whenever she was away from home, and her father usually added a lengthy P.S. to each letter. Charlie had promised to write, too, and so had Dr. Joe and Midge. She had written a hurried note to Gwen and Josie before leaving Hilton, telling them about her new assignment and had expected a reply early in the week. But although it seemed as though the mail pouch which Torry brought back from Tucson every morning was filled with letters for everyone else, Cherry had not even received a postcard.

The mailboxes, labeled with the name of everyone who was connected with the hacienda, lined one wall of the office. It was Mr. Conrad who sorted the mail and put the letters in their proper pigeonholes. The box labeled "Ames" had so far collected nothing but dust.

A wave of homesickness engulfed Cherry. Things wouldn't have seemed so bad if only she could have received one word from somebody who loved her. Another disappointment was the fact that she had not been able to keep the Tuesday evening date with Kirk Monroe after all. At the last minute, just as they were about to leave the hacienda, Señora had informed her coldly that Harold Bean had gone off an hour earlier and would not be back until midnight.

"Well, that's too darn bad!" Kirk had exploded. "Send somebody after him and make him come back. He knew Cherry had a date with me. It was all arranged."

"I can't help that," Señora had replied with a shrug of her slim shoulders. "Is it my fault that he is an absent-minded professor? I didn't know he had gone until I found this note on my desk saying that he had a seminar this evening. He also says, Miss Ames, that he informed you of this fact. So I simply do not understand why you didn't telephone Dr. Monroe and cancel your engagement with him."

"Is that true, Cherry?" Kirk asked.

"No, it's not true," Cherry had replied bluntly. "He hardly spoke a word to me the whole day."

"Have you looked in your mailbox?" Señora asked.

"Not since before lunch," Cherry said. "I know that Mr. Conrad distributes the mail between eleven and eleven-thirty. Since there was nothing in my box at noon it never occurred to me to look again." She hurried across the living room and into the office. Sure enough, in her box was a small piece of paper and on it were the words:

"Ames: Sorry. Have an important seminar this P.M. Better luck next time. H. B."

Anger made Cherry's cheeks flame. The tutor had covered himself by scribbling this note and putting it in her box. But at the same time he must have known that she would not look into her pigeonhole on the wall until noon of the following day.

She turned to Kirk and Señora who had followed her into the office. "All right," she said. "It's my fault. I didn't know that the mailboxes were used by the staff for the exchange of memos. I—"

"But, my dear Miss Ames," Señora interrupted, "you were informed of that yesterday. Harold Bean explained the details of our routine to you before lunch. I remember distinctly seeing you two standing in front of the fireplace for ten or fifteen minutes before the gong sounded. It was then that Harold explained to you, among other things, that we do use the mailboxes for intramural communications." She added to Kirk, "Miss Ames, I'm afraid, has allowed the attentions of our handsome young foreman to turn her head. It is only natural that she should be flustered by his obvious infatuation for her. But I'm sure her forgetfulness is only temporary and that she will soon settle down into the routine." She swept out of the office, her black eyes twinkling.

Cherry had known that there was no point in trying to tell Señora the truth. She obviously thought the world of Harold Bean, and her attitude toward Cherry had grown steadily colder and colder. The twins continued to be rude, and although not flagrantly disobedient, they constantly put Cherry in the disagreeable position of a stern martinet. Richie and Davie caused her no trouble and were even friendly when they reported to her daily for their vitamin capsules. But in the presence of the twins they ignored her. Nancy vacillated: she seemed very grateful to Cherry for encouraging her to stick to the slimming diet, but during the long stretch between lunch and dinner when she suffered from the pangs of hunger, she was often cross and accused Cherry of starving her into a state of malnutrition.

The members of the Foursome were always courteous and considerate, but, preoccupied with themselves, and having no need for medical attention, they paid scant attention to the nurse. Mrs. Blair grew more sarcastic by the day. Although she spent most of her time in her room, she demanded constant attention from the young Mexican maids and gleaned from them anything which might be considered gossip. And every fact Mrs. Blair gleaned she purposely misconstrued.

She had obviously learned that Cherry had not been able to keep her date with the young doctor on Tuesday night. But her version of it was that Kirk had broken the date because at the last minute he had been asked to dine at the home of a rich patient. Mrs. Blair knew, too, that Torry spent as much time with Cherry as he possibly could, and that Cherry frequently tried to avoid him in order to prevent gossip. But never a day passed without the old woman saying to Cherry:

"Well, having lost the doctor, you've set your cap for the foreman! I wouldn't think of asking you to rub my aching back. It might make your pretty hands red and rough."

But Cherry could take Mrs. Blair in her stride now. She honestly felt sorry for her and went out of her way to make this patient's life as pleasant and comfortable as she could. Whenever Mrs. Blair said, with biting sarcasm, "Don't bother to do so-and-so," Cherry always cheerfully did whatever Mrs. Blair told her not to do. But the querulous old woman never showed the slightest sign of gratitude.

And someone—probably the twins—continued to play pranks . . . always the kind of prank which meant that Cherry got the blame. Twice, shortly after Cherry put the Do Not Disturb sign on Mrs. Blair's door, it was taken off. A jam pot was substituted for Mrs. Blair's hairpin box with disastrous results. Her little brass dinner bell disappeared and reappeared inside her ice bag. Only the night before she had been rudely awakened out of a sound sleep when an alarm clock went off under her bed.

On that occasion, Cherry flatly refused to take the blame. The other pranks, by stretching the imagination, could have been checked up to carelessness on her part. But, as she told Señora hotly, when at last the furore had died down, "that clock was set and placed there deliberately. You can't possibly believe that a registered nurse would do such a thing. Why, it might have brought on a severe attack."

For once Señora sided with Cherry. "No one is accusing you, my dear," she said. "The clock was placed there by one of the Longman twins. I shall speak to them severely in the morning."

Of course she didn't speak to them severely, but she did say something which only made matters worse. At breakfast that morning Jacqueline greeted Cherry with:

"Tattletale-tit. I hope you have a fit."

Patty came quickly to Cherry's rescue. "Don't be silly, Jackie. Nobody tattled on you. Everyone knows you put that alarm clock under Mrs. Blair's bed. It's just the kind of mean, silly trick you and Johnny are forever playing on people. Like taking my letter and key." She shook her fist across the table at the twins. "You'd better stop going into other people's rooms unless you're asked. If you don't watch out you'll end up in jail."

Jacqueline's face turned white then red. "I never!" she yelled. "Never. *Never*. NEVER! I wouldn't put my foot in your horrible old cell even if you asked me to." She began to cry, and by the time Cherry reached her side she was coughing.

"Never mind," Cherry began, but before she could say another word, Señora was there, too. Everyone was staring at the teen-age table, and except for Jacqueline's choking coughs, there was utter silence. Even Harold Bean stopped with a spoonful of cereal halfway to his mouth.

Jacqueline threw her arms around Señora. "She said I was a thief," she gasped. "Take me to my room. I feel as though I were going to—" her voice died away into a rasping cough.

With a glance at Cherry, Señora led the girl out into the patio. Cherry followed. Surely Señora's glance had meant that she was going to need help. But hardly had Cherry closed the doors behind her when Señora said over one shoulder:

"Please return to the table, Miss Ames. And at least make some attempt to assist Mr. Bean in keeping the other teen-agers in a semblance of order."

Jacqueline had not had an attack. In fact, she had eaten a hearty breakfast in her room and had gone to the morning classes just as though nothing had happened. Nobody, not even Señora, had any comment to make about the breakfast-table scene.

Now that the day was over, Cherry sat alone in her room thinking over the week's events. Perhaps Jacqueline's frequent fits of temper at mealtimes were part of the routine. Perhaps the pranks were, too. And all of the other things that Cherry found so difficult to cope with. It was just a question of getting used to the routine.

"And my bad luck can't keep up," Cherry comforted herself. "Tomorrow we'll find Patty's nest egg. Or anyway, another clue."

CHAPTER XI

Another Disappointment

AND THEY DID! RIGHT AFTER BREAKFAST, CHERRY AND
Torry and Patty rode out to The Castle. They searched
it from top to bottom without finding so much as a shred
of a clue, but Cherry refused to be discouraged.

As she and Patty helped Torry fix lunch, barbecued
short ribs with a delicious Mexican sauce which he had
brought along in a jar, Cherry said:

"We found one note in a secret hiding place. So there
are probably other notes. When we find the right one
it'll tell us where the nest egg is hidden."

"It all seems so involved," Patty said dismally. "If
there is a nest egg why didn't Daddy tell me where it
was in the letter?"

"He didn't dare do that," Cherry said, "because some
dishonest person might have got hold of the letter be-

fore you did. So I think he did the next best thing. He left clues in the letter to where other clues were hidden."

Torry began to serve the food on paper plates. "I think you may have something there, Cherry," he said after they had eaten in silence for a while. "The word *bed* led you to the hollow four-poster legs. Maybe there's one word in the note we found last week that will lead us to another note."

"That's what I was thinking," Cherry said. "I thought maybe we ought to stick to nouns." She took the note from the brown envelope and said, "The nouns are *riser, man, way, top, ladder, step* and *step*. M-m-m. *Ladder* could mean the circular staircase which winds its *way* up to the balcony. It was built by a *man*. Oh," she interrupted herself. "Something may be hidden behind the riser between the two top steps."

They raced inside and up to the top steps of the staircase. "No secret hiding place there," Torry said.

"I don't even know what a riser is," Patty complained.

"They're the vertical pieces between the steps," he explained. "The uprights, in other words."

"Step by step," Cherry said suddenly as they reached the bottom step, "could mean the riser between the first and second step."

"A perfect secret hiding place," Torry agreed. He stooped. "*If* the riser should slide out. And," he finished in a shout, "*it does!*"

"And there's a note there, too," Patty cried excitedly. She reached over Torry's head to snatch up the scrap of paper. Cherry could see that the words had been written in the same spidery handwriting.

" 'My darling daughter,' " Patty read slowly. " 'Remember that your father was a champion pole vaulter in college, but he never let athletics interfere with his studies. I spent many hours at my desk, for I knew that "Knowledge is power." ' "

She stared at Cherry, her eyes wide with surprise. "But this couldn't have been written by Daddy, although it is his handwriting. He never went to college."

"That's true," Cherry and Torry said in unison.

"Oh, I give up," Patty moaned. "Daddy must have been—well, sort of crazy when he wrote this one."

Cherry couldn't help thinking the same thing, but she said cheerfully, "Let's not give up so easily. What your father wrote isn't important. It's the clues that are hidden in his messages that are important. He may have written about pole vaulting and college for a special reason."

"It's over my head," Torry said. "Pole vaulting and college can't have anything to do with where the nest egg is hidden." He started for the door with Patty trotting beside him.

"Wait a minute," Cherry begged them. "*College* and *studies* and *desk* and *knowledge* all go together. And they must mean that Patty should search his desk."

"We *have* searched it," Patty said. "You can try, if you like, Cherry, but there isn't anything there."

Cherry wandered over to stare at the strange-looking piece of furniture. It was made of cholla cactus wood and four big thumbtacks marked the rectangle where a blotter must once have been. The desk was honey-combed with pigeonholes and tiny drawers. A quick glance assured her that the pigeonholes were empty.

"There's nothing in the drawers either," Torry told her with elaborate patience. "Nor behind them, nor under them. We took every single one out, didn't we, Patty?"

Patty nodded. "And there isn't any other place to look. Don't you see now, Cherry, that it isn't really a separate piece of furniture? It is merely a space between two joists, and the boards forming the desk are attached to the walls of the bookcases on both sides."

"Oh, it's probably attached to a beam in the back, too," Torry said. "But that gets us nowhere. Come on, Cherry, let's go. It's the opening day of La Fiesta de los Vaqueros—the Cowboy Festival. It's the most colorful rodeo in the world. You'll see champions thrown by broncs and Brahma bulls. Bull riding, calf roping, and bulldogging, too."

"What's bulldogging?" Cherry asked.

"Wrestling with a steer. Come on. We've already

missed the parade." He took Cherry's arm and tucked it in the crook of his arm. "You're due for a good time. Don't think I don't know what a tough time you've been having at the ranch."

"She certainly has," Patty agreed. "You'll love the rodeo, Cherry."

Cherry let them lead her outside. There really wasn't any other place to look in The Castle. They cantered back toward the ranch, following the old wagon road. "We didn't leave a stone unturned," she said sorrowfully. "Oh, maybe I should have said we didn't leave a *tile* unturned! Did you go over every inch of the floor carefully, Patty? Are you positive none of the tiles is loose?"

"Positive," Patty said.

"How could you be positive?" Cherry asked dubiously. "There must be dozens of them. How do you know you didn't test the same ones twice and skip others?"

"Because," Patty explained, "I marked each one with a piece of chalk. Then Torry checked me to make sure that every tile had a chalk mark on it."

"That's right," Torry said with a chuckle. "She did skip a lot, too. And I marked those with chalk, then she checked me."

Patty giggled. "He skipped a few, too, but in the end, although we were both dizzy, we didn't miss one."

When they arrived at the corral they dismounted and Torry said to Cherry, "See you in five minutes. This is one time you can wear lipstick and powder, although you don't need either. But otherwise, don't change your costume in any way. During the Cowboy Festival everyone in Tucson wears just what you've got on now. Plus a ten-gallon hat. Bill will be honored to lend you his."

Cherry and Patty hurried toward the patio. "Please have fun," Patty said. "Forget about me and my nest egg and those horrid twins and that mean old Mrs. Blair."

Cherry stopped short in her tracks. "Oh, Patty, you don't mean that. Mrs. Blair is old and sick—at least, she thinks she's sick, which amounts to the same thing. I feel sorry for the twins, too, not because they're asthmatics—they'll outgrow that—but because their mother doesn't seem to care much about them. She sends them expensive presents, but she hardly ever writes or calls them up. And all their father seems to do is to pay their bills."

"Oh, stop being such a Pollyanna," Patty cried impatiently. "I used to feel sorry for Jackie and Johnny, too. It's their own fault that they don't get a lot of letters from home. They never write to their mother unless Señora makes them do it. I'll bet if they wrote her nice letters she'd answer every one. They claim she doesn't care anything about them, but maybe she thinks they don't care anything about her. Just because she's a famous movie actress doesn't mean she isn't a human being. And I know their father is awfully good to them."

"She's probably awfully busy, though," Cherry said, "and that explains why she doesn't write more often. My own mother is busy, too, but I've been feeling so blue because I haven't heard from her since I left home a week ago that I planned to call her up tonight. Silly of me. After all, I've been on duty in plenty of places where I *couldn't* get letters from home for weeks at a time."

"But not in places like this where everyone has made you so miserable," Patty said stormily. "I just don't understand Señora. She's really a lovely person, Cherry. And she knows how much trouble Mrs. Blair and the twins cause every nurse we've ever had. She's not cold to you on account of them. She feels the same way about them that you do; she feels sorry for them. This is the only home they've ever had. Otherwise, she wouldn't let them be guests. But she does realize that they're awful nuisances."

"Oh," Cherry said without thinking, "I thought— I mean, I somehow got the impression that she felt that they were an important factor in the ranch's profits."

Patty sniffed. "I don't know who gave you that impression. Señora could rent those suites to a lot of other people. Uncle Frank has to turn down star boarders every fall. Mr. Longman and a lot of other people wanted to rent my suite all the year round before I—I gave it up." She tossed her head. "I didn't mind giving it up. I never needed two rooms. It was just that Daddy wanted to be sure that the room Johnny has now was always ready for him. Sometimes he arrived for a visit without even sending a telegram first. And I don't mind having to go to work either instead of finishing high school. That's what Daddy wanted me to do. That's why he wrote me those letters. All three of them said pretty much the same thing: 'Start at the bottom and work your way up to the top, Patty!' "

She ran off along the path, darted across the patio, and inside the house. Cherry followed more slowly. Patty was trying to be brave, but she hadn't fooled Cherry.

"She counted on me to help her find the nest egg," Cherry thought dismally. "And I failed her. I've been a failure at everything I've tried ever since I came to Arizona."

"*Cherry!*"

Cherry turned. Torry was hurrying along the path after her. "For Pete's sake," he said when he caught up with her. "You haven't even washed your face let alone put on your war paint. There are cobwebs in your hair or have you turned gray in the last five minutes?" He bowed and plunked a ten-gallon hat on top of her head. "But I'm not fussy, Calamity Jane. On you, cobwebs look good." He crooked his arm at her. "My own special gasoline-age bucking bronco, commonly known as a Model A Ford, awaits us yonder. The key is always in the lock because nobody would have it as a gift, and there is always a flashlight in the door pocket in case we have to proceed on foot."

Cherry laughed. Torry was so gay and gallant she couldn't help forgetting that she was a dismal failure as a ranch nurse. Just for this one afternoon and evening she *would* have fun.

And then it happened. Señora suddenly appeared on the patio. "Oh, Cherry," she called, cupping her slim brown hands gracefully, "I'm so glad I caught you, my dear." She moved swiftly across the patio and down the path. "I'm terribly sorry, my dear, but I can't let you have the evening off after all. While you were out riding, Harold Bean received a call from the University. A special seminar, I gather. At any rate, he just left."

"Special seminar," Torry said, biting out every syllable as though the wind had blown sand into his mouth. "On a Sunday? The opening day of La Fiesta de los Vaqueros? Honestly, Señora, I can't understand why you let him get by with that kind of thing?" He turned to Cherry. "If you have a grain of sense in your head you'll quit and keep your date with me."

Cherry was sorely tempted to follow Torry's advice. For Harold Bean to play the same trick on her twice in one week was too much. For it was a trick, Cherry was convinced, and a mean one. All of her unhappiness came flooding back. This job was just too difficult; there was no point in trying to cope with the unfair situations that kept arising. She might as well resign now and get it over with.

Then suddenly Cherry thought of Dr. Joe, and she could see his sensitive, beautiful face and his luminous eyes. He had gone through long periods of discouragement when everything and everyone had seemed to be against him, but he had never given up.

Cherry forced herself to smile at Señora. "I am disappointed," she admitted, "but it can't be helped." She took the big hat from her head and gave it back to the young foreman who was obviously seething with rage. "I'm sorry, Torry."

Señora went back into the house and he said bitterly, "Go ahead and be a Caspar Milquetoast if you like, but I'm not going to let Bean get by with this!" He strode away leaving her forlornly alone on the path.

CHAPTER XII

~~~~~~

An Unpleasant Scene

CHERRY WENT TO HER ROOM, SHOWERED, AND CHANGED
into a fresh uniform. Then she realized that it was the
only clean one she had left. She had given the others to
the Mexican laundress on Saturday and would not receive them back until Monday morning after breakfast.
If there was any delay, Cherry would not have a stiffly
starched uniform to wear while she made the rounds
with Dr. Monroe.

"Take no chances, Calamity Jane," Cherry said to
herself as she took off her uniform and hung it in the
closet. "Since you're not officially on duty today, you can
wear anything you like. M-m-m. Now what *do* you like?
Humor yourself, Calammy. You deserve it." Looking
over her scant wardrobe reminded Cherry of the fact

that she had nothing to wear at dinner that evening. She had given her one and only long-skirted frock to the laundress, too, feeling sure that the dresses she had asked her mother to send her would arrive on Monday. All week Cherry had treasured that O.A.O. frock, taking it off right after dinner. Throughout the meal she had lived in fear and trembling for fear Harold Bean's clumsiness and the twins' bad table manners would result in an accident that would mean the gown would have to be washed and ironed right away.

Cherry would have preferred doing all her own laundry, but had learned early in the week that it was strictly against the rules.

"You may, of course, swoosh out your undies and stockings," Señora had answered her question. "But there just isn't any place near the hacienda where larger pieces could be hung out to dry without becoming an eyesore. If I allowed you to set up a temporary clothesline between the two mounds outside the kitchen door, the occupants of the cabins would soon follow suit." Clasping her hands with horror, she had finished, "Why, in no time at all this place would look like the back yards in the Mexican Quarter."

So Cherry had dismissed the laundry problem from her mind. At that time she had felt secure in the thought that a box of evening frocks from her mother would arrive on Saturday at the latest. Even when the box didn't arrive she hadn't worried because she had counted on having the twenty-four hours off from Sunday after breakfast to Monday after breakfast.

But now, due to Harold Bean, she had to have something suitable to wear at dinner that evening. That meant borrowing from Patty. Cherry didn't want to borrow from Patty. Boots were one thing; an expensive frock which could be ruined by an indelible stain was quite different. So far as their wardrobes were concerned, Patty was in the same boat that Harold Bean had found himself in three years ago. Unless Patty found her nest egg, it would be a long, long time before she could replenish her wardrobe.

"And," Cherry reflected, "if I accidentally ruined the dress I borrowed from her, it would be months before I could save enough money to buy her another one." For Cherry knew that those "simple, little frocks" in Patty's closet had come from stores where the prices started at one hundred dollars. When Patty had made her try them on, Cherry had seen the labels. They had fit beautifully, except for the length of the skirts, most of which had wide hems that could easily be let out and pressed with the small iron Cherry always carried with her.

Cherry paced the floor, feeling like a prisoner in a cell. "Never a borrower nor a lender be" was a good motto. But so was "When in Rome, do as the Romans do."

Finally Cherry made up her mind. Willy-nilly, she would wear the skirt of her suit with a pretty white Nylon blouse. If she stuck out like a sore thumb in the dining room that evening it wasn't her fault.

And she might have slipped in and out of the dining room without attracting attention if it hadn't been for the twins. Cherry didn't even have a chance to sit down before Jacqueline said in a loud voice to Nancy:

"If one of us came to the table in sports clothes we'd catch it! But you notice the nurse can wear anything she likes and get by with it."

Cherry remained standing and said firmly in a clear voice: "It so happens, Jacqueline Longman, that the only evening dress I brought with me is in the laundry. As you know, I am officially off duty today. So please make no further comments about what I am wearing."

Jacqueline stared at her in surprise. Cherry had never spoken to her in that crisp tone of voice before. The other teen-agers stared at Cherry, too. Nancy giggled nervously. Patty, who had been filling the water glasses at the other tables, joined them then. She stared, too; first at Cherry and then at Harold Bean's empty place.

"Why, Cherry," she cried, "what are you doing here? You're supposed to be at the Cowboy Festival."

"Never mind," Cherry began, but before she could say another word, Richie spoke up:

"Yeah, how about that? Torry told me himself that

he had a date with you, Miss Ames. Where's Harold Bean, anyway?"

"That's right," Davie said, frowning. "That guy's getting to be a regular Mexican jumping bean. Now you see him, and now you don't. Did he sneak out and leave you in the lurch as he did last Tuesday, Miss Ames?"

"Oh, how mean of him," Nancy put in. "I always said he was a sneaky old scarecrow. He's supposed to be in the classroom every evening to help us, but you notice he never is. That's why I get such bad marks. You, too, Jackie. He's never around when we want to ask him some questions about algebra, is he? Why isn't he?"

Patty slid into her chair. "That's what I want to know. What right has he got to go off whenever he feels like it?"

"Never mind," Cherry began again, but this time she was interrupted by Jacqueline who said:

"It's her own fault she got stuck. If Miss Ames had left the hacienda right after breakfast the way the other nurses did, Harold couldn't have sneaked out. But you notice she hung around." She leaned forward and asked Nancy pointedly: "Do you know why? Because she's in love with Torry, that's why."

It was all so silly that Cherry couldn't help laughing. "I'm not in love with anyone, Jackie," she said quietly. "And you're right. It *is* my own fault that I got stuck. On my next day off I *will* leave right after breakfast, since that seems to be the only way that a nurse can guarantee a holiday for herself."

Jacqueline sneered. "There won't be another day off for you. If you're still here next Sunday, I'll—I'll eat my ten-gallon hat."

Anger surged through Cherry's amusement. "That will do, Jacqueline," she said sternly. "From now on there will be no more personal remarks made at this table. If anyone breaks that rule I shall ask him or her to leave."

No one said anything for a long, dreary ten minutes. Then Johnny Longman broke the silence with a loud laugh. "It's like that game: 'The next one who speaks is a monkey.' What's the matter with us? Can't we think of anything to say that isn't personal?" He clasped his forehead with both hands in mock despair. "Oh, gosh, I guess I was being personal then—talking about us."

Everyone joined in his laughter and Cherry thought: "Johnny really is a nice boy and he has a grand sense of humor. If it weren't for Jacqueline, he and I could be friends. And vice versa. If only I could do something to make Johnny approve of me, Jacqueline might at least listen to me long enough for me to prove to her that I *am* a twin and *not* a tattletale."

But what could a Calamity Jane do to make anyone approve of her? Nothing, Cherry decided. Not until my streak of bad luck runs out.

The waitress was passing the dessert now; big slices of lemon meringue pie. Nancy was stunned when she received a portion as large as the others. "Oh, no, Cherry," she cried. "Not for me. Pie is fattening."

"You're being personal," Jacqueline said sharply.

Cherry ignored her. "You've been so good about not eating sweets between meals," she told Nancy, "that you can have anything you like for dessert from now on. Besides, it's only the crust of lemon meringue pie that's fattening."

"Golly, golly, golly." Nancy's eyes were as big as saucers. "Giving up candy wasn't nearly as bad as I thought it was going to be. But I couldn't have done it, Cherry, if you hadn't helped me. Gee," she finished, "thanks."

"Leave the table, Nancy," Jacqueline said loudly. "And if Miss Ames were honest, she'd leave too. Both of you have made about ten personal remarks in the last three minutes."

"So what?" Davie demanded. "Diet is part of a nurse's job, and it also has a lot to do with eating, in case you're interested. That kind of personal remark has just got to be said."

"It sure does," Richie heartily agreed. "Gleeps. Suppose we couldn't say 'Please may I have a second helping'? Davie and I would soon be as skinny as Harold Bean."

"Now *you're* being personal," Jacqueline said airily.

"Oh, stop it, Jackie," Patty cried impatiently. "You made a personal remark about Miss Ames. And I just made one about you, so I guess we'd all better leave the table."

"Not Johnny," Jacqueline said fiercely. "He didn't say a word."

"I'm through, anyway," Johnny said easily.

Davie howled with laughter. "You're in the same boat now with the rest of us. Oh, gosh, Miss Ames, what can we do to keep from making personal remarks?"

Everyone was laughing now except Jacqueline. "I guess I was wrong," Cherry finally got out. "What I really meant to say was that it's very rude to say disagreeable things to or about a person, especially if that person happens to be present. Being disagreeable at mealtimes isn't good for your digestion, and it isn't good either for the digestion of the person whose feelings you have hurt. So let's modify the rule. No more *rude* personal remarks at the table. Okay?"

"Okay," Davie and Richie agreed. Nancy and Patty nodded, and Johnny finally said, "Suits me."

"Well, it doesn't suit me," Jacqueline said with a toss of her head. "If I agreed, it would be the same thing as admitting that I was rude to Miss Ames."

"You were rude," Patty said quickly. "And I don't care if I have broken the rule by telling you so to your face. I was leaving, anyway, to go wash the silver, so please may I be excused now?" She left, her head high.

"You're all excused," Cherry said and led the way out to the patio.

Not until then did she realize that Torry had been right to call her a Caspar Milquetoast. Ignoring Jacqueline's pranks and rude remarks had not improved their relationship. Perhaps if she treated the twins as though she were a strict governess they might behave better. Heretofore, because she knew that Jacqueline was subject to attacks, Cherry had been lenient. And so, of course, Jackie had taken advantage of her.

"I should have sent her from the table the very first time she was rude to me," Cherry admitted to herself. "I *was* a Milquetoast, but no more."

And then she heard the loud-speaker blaring: "Miss Ames. Nurse Ames. Please go to Mrs. Blair. Mrs. Blair."

Cherry hurried inside and tapped on the old woman's door.

"Come in." Mrs. Blair was propped up in bed, but she was breathing naturally. "I sent for you, Miss Ames," she said, "because I have been left in this position ever since my dinner tray was taken away. I am most uncomfortable, but I wouldn't think of asking you to lower my head and remove some of the pillows. I merely wished you to—" She stopped and glared at Cherry who was calmly adjusting the bed. "What do you mean by coming in here without your uniform?"

Cherry smiled and gently took two of the pillows from under her head. Deftly she plumped up the other one and replaced it. "I'm not officially on duty, Mrs. Blair. And even if I were on duty I wouldn't be in uniform at this moment. Señora requires that I wear an evening gown at dinner."

"Well, then," the old woman demanded, "why aren't you in an evening gown?"

"Because," Cherry said again, "I'm not officially on duty."

"Don't be impertinent," Mrs. Blair snapped. "If you are not on duty, what are you doing here?"

"You sent for me," Cherry replied cheerfully. "You really should have asked for one of the maids, but I don't mind. Is there anything else I can do?"

Mrs. Blair said nothing, so Cherry left and started across the living room to her own cubbyhole. Again the loud-speaker blared her name:

"Miss Ames. Please report to the office."

"Now what?" Cherry asked herself. Were the Conrads going to reprimand her for wearing a blouse and skirt at dinner? If so, she was not going to be a Milquetoast, no matter what the consequences might be. It was officially her day off, so she had a perfect right to wear what she pleased. Holding her head high, she marched into the office.

CHAPTER XIII

A Cruel Joke

IT WAS FRANK CONRAD WHO HAD CALLED CHERRY ON the intercom, and she had expected to find him and Señora waiting for her in the office. But instead of Señora, Cherry discovered, to her surprise, that Torry Torrington was there. The two men stood up as she came in and Frank Conrad said without any preamble, "Miss Ames, Torry has been telling me about what happened this afternoon. I also understand that Harold Bean left you in the lurch on Tuesday. Why didn't you complain to me?"

Cherry sat down in the nearest chair. She had expected an angry scene and here was Frank Conrad standing up for her.

"I never thought about complaining to anyone,"

Cherry said. "I took it for granted that it was more important for Harold Bean to attend a seminar than it was for me to keep my date."

"Seminar, indeed!" Frank Conrad exploded. "He's all through with seminars. He finished his academic work last year. If he doesn't settle down soon and do some writing he'll never get that thesis done. I understood that was why he took this position in the first place. So he could write up his notes. But that's beside the point." He pounded on the desk. "The point is that your day off has been ruined. So forget that it was supposed to be your day off. As soon as you have made the rounds with the doctor tomorrow morning you are free to do as you please until Tuesday morning at nine."

"Oh, that wouldn't be fair to Señora," Cherry protested. "She's done all of the nursing chores today. I really haven't done a thing."

Frank Conrad pounded the desk again. "You've made yourself available, though. I heard Mrs. Blair calling you on the intercom only a few minutes ago. If you didn't consider yourself officially on duty before, consider yourself so now." He smiled broadly. "Get into uniform, run around with thermometers and ice bags if you must for the sake of your conscience, but forget that this was your day off." He turned to Torry. "How am I doing?"

"Fine," Torry said. "That's the only way to talk to her. She's a Milquetoast."

Cherry laughed. "Well, thank you very much, Mr. Conrad. If you're sure it's all right with Señora . . ."

"Let me speak for myself."

Cherry wheeled. Señora was standing at the entrance to the Conrads' suite which opened into the office. She was wearing a ravishingly beautiful evening gown, lipstick, powder, and rouge. As she spoke, she daubed perfume behind her ears. Chuckling, she said to Cherry, "It isn't often Frank and I get a chance to go out on a Sunday evening. And it's been ages since I've used any cosmetics. I'm really glad that you're going to have tomorrow off instead of today."

It was all too much for Cherry. Everyone had been against her and now they all seemed to be on her side. Was it possible that Calamity Jane's luck was changing?

Cherry hurried across the living room and out to the patio to cool her burning cheeks. Torry followed close on her heels.

"What you need," he said, "is your own special foreman. Someone to manage you." He took off his jacket and placed it around her shoulders. "A sure way to catch pneumonia is to forget that it gets cold in Arizona at this time of the year after sundown."

The rising moon flooded the terrace with a silvery light, and the shadows cast by the twin mounds near the kitchen door were weird purple blotches. In the blue-black sky there were about a million more twinkling stars than Cherry had ever seen before in her whole life.

"It's all so beautiful," she said, more to herself than to Torry. "I can't imagine now why I felt so lonely and unhappy such a short time ago."

"You had every reason to feel that way," he said gruffly. "As I told you almost exactly a week ago, this job is tough. Even without Harold Bean it would be plenty tough, but he's making the situation impossible for you. For two cents I'd give him a poke in the jaw."

"Oh, he's not so bad," Cherry said, smiling. "Just thoughtless and absent-minded."

"That's what *you* think," he said emphatically. "That guy is out to get you fired. I don't know why. If he had any sense he'd realize it's a break for him having you here. I gather from Davie and Richie that you're doing a lot of his chores for him. Like making sure the kids rest after lunch and that they're all in bed with lights out at ten o'clock. And he's supposed to be available during their evening study period, but every evening after dinner I see him drive off in that midget car of his. How does he fold himself into that little thing, anyway?"

Cherry laughed. "It's a mystery to me why such a long-legged man chose a midget to drive around in. But it's none of our business. And I still don't see why you think he wants me to leave."

"You will," he replied. "He's been telling Señora that you resent being treated as though you were a governess.

He gave her the impression that you were forever complaining to him. I tried to correct that impression, but I'm not sure that I succeeded. She's known him on and off most of his life, and she's only known you for a week."

"That's funny," Cherry said thoughtfully. "He's forever telling me that I shouldn't let Señora take advantage of me. I guess you're right, Torry. He wants me to leave, but why?"

He shrugged. "You're the detective."

"I'm beginning to wonder," Cherry continued, "if maybe he's the one who has been playing some of the pranks—not the twins. Some of the more serious ones, I mean. Like taking Mrs. Blair's sheet from the Doctor's Order Book. Well, anyway," she finished, "I can't stand out here worrying about Harold Bean. I've got to get into uniform."

"Okay," he said. "But tomorrow's a date. Don't let anything interfere with that."

Cherry gave him back his jacket and hurried inside. The moment she opened her door she realized that she was still a Calamity Jane. The whole room reeked of her favorite brand of perfume. She glanced at the atomizer on her bureau. It was almost empty.

In a panic she yanked open her closet door. Here the fragrance was almost overpowering. Someone, not so long ago, had sprayed every garment she owned with perfume. And her one and only clean uniform was still damp with it. At the same moment Cherry heard the loud-speaker blare her name:

"Miss Ames. Nurse Ames. Please go to Mrs. Blair. Urgent. Miss Ames . . ."

"Oh, oh," Cherry moaned as she darted across the living room. "Now I am in for it. Señora must have told Mrs. Blair that I would be on duty tonight. What excuse can I give her for not being in uniform?"

CHAPTER XIV

A Midnight Scare

TOO LATE CHERRY REALIZED THAT INVESTIGATING THE contents of her closet had been a mistake. She didn't exactly reek of perfume, but a faint aroma followed her into Mrs. Blair's room like an invisible black cloud of doom. To make matters worse, one glance at the patient told Cherry that Mrs. Blair was on the verge of having a mild attack.

The old woman was breathing with difficulty, but when she saw and smelled Cherry, her rate of respiration increased alarmingly.

Cherry hastily adjusted the bed so that she was in the High Fowler's position.

"You—you—" Mrs. Blair gasped, pointing a shaking finger. "You're on duty . . . you're not in uniform

. . . you reek of perfume . . . Get out! You'll be the death of me!"

If only Señora were here to take over for a few minutes! Forcing herself to be calm, Cherry washed her hands—the hands which had touched her perfume-drenched uniform! Then she said into the intercom:

"Send a maid to Mrs. Blair at once. A maid to Mrs. Blair. This is Nurse Ames. Urgent."

The patient was choking and gasping now. Cherry didn't dare leave her alone while she went for the medication, tourniquet, and the hypodermic syringe. And yet Mrs. Blair must have an intravenous injection of aminophylline right away. Where were all the maids?

Someone tapped on the door, and Patty poked her head inside. "All of the maids are at the rodeo," she said. "Can I help?"

"Yes, yes," Cherry said, pushing past her into the living room. "Stay with Mrs. Blair until I come back."

The keys to the Nurse's Station were, of course, in the toe of her riding boot way back on the floor of that contaminated closet. Getting them meant brushing head and shoulders against the reeking clothes. But it couldn't be helped.

Once inside the station, Cherry hurriedly opened the container where a supply of sterile syringes were always kept ready for an emergency. To her horror she realized at once that the numbers on the syringes did not match the numbers on the plungers. Another prank—a serious prank. Someone had been in the Nurse's Station since she had checked the supplies before going off duty that morning. Someone had deliberately mixed up those syringes and plungers.

This meant more delay because the hypodermics were now no longer sterile. A delay of even three minutes could mean that Mrs. Blair might not respond to the injection. In that case she would have to be given a mixture of oxygen and helium in a hurry.

Cherry plugged in the sterilizer. Those three minutes seemed like three hundred years. But at last she was back in Mrs. Blair's room. The patient, thank heavens, was no worse. In fact, she seemed calmer.

Patty helped Cherry apply the tourniquet and said in her soothing young voice, "Now, try to relax, Mrs. Blair. Why don't you close your eyes or face the wall? Lie as quietly as you can . . . Miss Ames can't hurry this injection, you know. . . . Only five minutes more . . . just re-lax . . . There! It's all over now, and you're going to feel fine in a very short while."

Cherry gave Patty a grateful and admiring look. "The less I say to the patient the better," she thought ruefully. But she had to check Mrs. Blair's pulse and respiration. She could only hope that Mrs. Blair was not as allergic to perfume as she thought she was. She had scrubbed her hands at the Nurse's Station, but she knew that before she would be completely rid of the clinging fragrance she would have to shampoo her hair and change her blouse.

Mrs. Blair glared at her wordlessly, but her eyes shot daggers. The effect of the injection was dramatic. In five minutes she was breathing easily; her pulse and respiration normal. Cherry released her wrist and retreated to a chair in the far corner of the room.

Busying herself with the chart, she said in as offhand a tone of voice as she could muster, "Now just rest quietly, Mrs. Blair. Don't try to talk."

The attack, although mild and brief, had apparently frightened the old woman into silence. She clung to Patty's hand, staring up at the ceiling. After a while her eyes closed, and she fell asleep.

Cherry tiptoed out into the living room, beckoning for Patty to follow her. "I'm going to spend the night with her," Cherry whispered. "Someone squirted perfume over everything in my closet . . ."

Patty looked horrified. "Oh, Cherry, how cruel!"

"*Sh-h*," Cherry cautioned her. "If you'll open the double doors in my room and hang my uniform between them, I think it may be all right so I can wear it tomorrow. I *have* to wear it when I make the rounds with Dr. Monroe."

Patty nodded. "I'll bring you one of my warm housecoats, Cherry. And the quilt from your bed. And don't worry about Lights Out for the kids. I'll check up on them for you. The twins are the only ones who ever disobey the rule, anyway. And when I tell Jackie what I think of her—!" She darted off.

Cherry waited inside the partially open door until she came back with the robe and quilt. "Thanks, honey," she whispered. "And listen, Patty, don't accuse Jackie of anything. One patient is all I can cope with until Señora comes back. It's ten o'clock now, on the button. If Jackie's light is still on, simply come back and report to me. You can tell by looking at the crack under her door. I'll wait here. If you don't come back in five minutes I'll know that all is well."

Leaving the door slightly ajar, Cherry took off her blouse and slipped on Patty's deliciously warm housecoat. Then she tiptoed into the bathroom, closed the door, rinsed the blouse in warm water and hung it over a towel rack to dry. Who could tell? She might have to wear it tomorrow. Thank goodness it was Nylon and didn't have to be ironed.

At 10:15 Cherry wrapped herself in the quilted comforter and curled up in the big overstuffed chair. Through the partially open door she could hear the voices of the Foursome. "I'll double Four Spades," she heard Mr. Neap say, and then suddenly it was midnight and the room was flooded by the moonlight which streamed through the window behind her.

Cherry had been dreaming that she had just dived off the deck of the *Julita* into a vast, cloying pool of perfume. But the odor that assailed her nostrils when she awoke was not that of perfume; it was the acrid smell that a too-hot iron makes when it comes in contact with a piece of damp cloth.

"Patty," Cherry thought with horror. "She probably decided to wash and iron my uniform for me and forgot to unplug the iron before she went to bed."

Mrs. Blair was sleeping peacefully. Cherry sped across the living room to her own cubbyhole. Halfway there, she skidded to a stop. The scorching odor was coming from the twins' suite. Cherry wheeled, tore back, and yanked open Jacqueline's door.

One quick glance told her what had happened. Jackie had not turned off her light at ten o'clock. Instead, in order to avoid detection, she had wrapped her towel around her bedside lamp. Then she must have fallen asleep. The weight of the towel had tilted the shade so that it had come in direct contact with the bulb, and the heat from the bulb had already reduced the lamp shade to a few scorched threads. If the towel had not been damp to begin with, the whole room might now be in flames. Flames which might have spread rapidly to the Nurse's Station where the oxygen tanks were stored!

Cherry turned off the lamp with a shaking hand. Then she gingerly lifted the scorched towel from the skeleton of the shade. Into the bathroom she carried it, dumped it into the basin, and filled the basin with water. Now there was no longer any danger of fire, so Cherry decided to leave the mess for Jackie to discover herself in the morning.

"Maybe the gruesome sight will teach her a lesson," Cherry thought as she hurried back to Mrs. Blair. The old woman had not stirred. Cherry checked her pulse and respiration, charted it as normal, then curled up in the chair to doze until morning.

She was awakened by the sound of Mrs. Blair's voice as she spoke into the intercom:

"Señora. Come to Mrs. Blair, please. Señora to Mrs. Blair."

"Oh, don't disturb Señora," Cherry cried. "It's only six o'clock and she and Mr. Conrad were out late last night."

"Leave me at once," the old lady cried petulantly.

Señora arrived then in dressing gown and slippers. She stared at Cherry and then at Mrs. Blair. "What on earth—?"

Cherry realized that her presence was only upsetting the patient, so she merely handed Señora the chart and departed.

Back in her own room she found to her surprise and delight that Patty had indeed washed her uniform the night before and was now ironing it.

"You angel," Cherry cried. "You shouldn't have done it."

"It was fun," Patty said with a giggle. "I had to put it through six rinse waters, so I knew I was right. Airing it all night wouldn't have done any good."

"I'll finish ironing it," Cherry said. "I'm used to this little folding ironing board. Oh, Patty, Mrs. Blair is telling Señora right now how I reeked of perfume last night. How can I ever explain that it wasn't my fault?"

"You can tell her the truth," Patty said briskly. "If you don't, I will. Jackie did it, of course. She was furious because you scolded her at lunch yesterday. She told me she was going to get even with you."

Cherry shook her head. "We have no way of proving it. Besides, I'm not a tattletale. But one thing is certain. My door is going to be locked whenever I leave my room from now on."

"Mine, too," Patty said. "And I'm also going to lock myself in at night. Cherry, somebody sneaked into my room around one o'clock this morning. Or anyway, tried to. I woke up just in time to see the door softly close." She shuddered reminiscently. "I was so scared for a moment I couldn't breathe. Then I jumped out of bed and ran out into the living room. Nobody was there, but I could see a shadow moving across the patio in the moonlight. It was horrible, Cherry. It looked like a giant daddy longlegs!"

CHAPTER XV

Cowboy Festival

DR. MONROE ARRIVED AT NINE AND GREETED CHERRY gaily. "It may be Blue Monday for some people," he said, "but, because it means I'm with you, it's my favorite day of the week."

"This is no time for compliments," Cherry said with a weary smile. "Mrs. Blair—"

But Señora joined them in the Nurse's Station then, and to Cherry's surprise she was in head-to-toe white. "I'll make the rounds with the doctor this morning, Miss Ames," she said coldly. "Mrs. Blair is still very upset because you were not in uniform last evening and were, furthermore, wearing perfume. I don't understand any of it, but she refused to allow you to enter her room. Jacqueline Longman is also upset. As you know, she had

154

breakfast in her room. She does not wish to see you."

"What's been happening around here?" Kirk broke in. "Cherry wearing perfume on duty? Ridiculous. How can you take seriously anything Blair says? And as for that spoiled youngster, Jackie Longman—what she needs is a good spanking."

Señora raised her black eyebrows. "As of now Miss Ames is off duty until tomorrow morning. She and I can discuss the various problems then. Good-by, Miss Ames."

Cherry hesitated. This was no time to make a special request, but it had to be done. "Before I leave, Señora," she said, "I should like to have a key to my room."

Señora narrowed her eyes. "There was a key in your door when you arrived last Sunday. Have you lost it?"

Cherry shook her head. "I'm sorry to contradict you, Señora, but there was no key in my door when I arrived."

Señora shrugged. "*I* shall not contradict *you*, but I put the key in the lock myself shortly before you arrived. However, you may obtain a duplicate from Mr. Conrad. Now, good morning, Miss Ames."

"Good morning," Cherry replied evenly, and marched out. She was fed to the teeth with the whole thing.

Frank Conrad, fortunately, was in the office. He greeted her pleasantly and gave her a key to her room without asking any questions. Cherry thanked him and went to her little cubbyhole to think things through. She had left her closet door open, hoping that eventually the breeze that swept in through the wide-open doors would rid it of its overpowering fragrance. It was closed now and she discovered to her horror that the Mexican laundress had been and gone.

She had hung in the closet all of Cherry's clean uniforms and her one and only evening gown. So now they too were contaminated. And then Cherry remembered that the only uncontaminated garment she owned, outside of the undies and stockings in her bureau drawers, was the Nylon blouse which she had left hanging on the towel rack in Mrs. Blair's bathroom.

Suddenly Cherry was overcome by laughter. The situation was so completely hopeless that it was ludicrous. Even the key which she had got from Mr. Conrad was useless. It was a duplicate and somebody else obviously had the one which Señora had placed in the lock a week ago. Señora, she was sure, had not made a mistake about that. Whoever had taken the key was her enemy. He or she—or they—had taken the Nurse's Station keys from her bureau drawer last week. He must have made wax impressions of the keys and had duplicates made. The same enemy had taken Mrs. Blair's sheet from the Doctor's Order Book and put it in the menu jacket. He had, undoubtedly, using his duplicate key to the Nurse's Station, mixed up the syringes and plungers yesterday.

There was a pattern in all of those "pranks." They had been done for the sole purpose of getting Cherry into serious trouble. The other pranks did not quite fit into the same category. They had, Cherry felt sure, been done thoughtlessly and on the spur of the moment by the twins.

An enemy! Cherry shivered involuntarily. It was not pleasant to know that someone whom she couldn't identify was doing everything possible to ruin her career. What his next step would be she couldn't even imagine.

Only one thought was comforting. There was nothing personal in this unknown's animosity. For reasons of his own, he had planned to get rid of her before she had even arrived at the hacienda. Why? The only fact he could have obtained about her at that time was that she was an experienced registered nurse.

Then suddenly she remembered that Kirk Monroe had told everyone beforehand that she also had a reputation as an amateur detective. Now it all made sense. Her enemy must be a criminal who feared that she might expose him. It made sense, but it still left the criminal, if he was one, an unknown. There were almost a hundred people, counting the guests and employees, who could be considered suspects, for although none of them apparently had a motive, all of them had the opportunity to play tricks on her. Trying to single out one would be like trying to find a needle in a haystack.

Cherry decided not to try. Chances were that Señora would ask her to resign tomorrow morning. The thing to do now was to air the clothes in her closet as best she could, get ready for her date with Torry, go to the Cowboy Festival, forget her troubles, and have a good time.

And Cherry did have a good time. She lost herself in the excitement of watching the various contests in the arena, "Whoopin' and hollerin'" with the other spectators, although, according to Torry, she invariably applauded contestants who, in his expert opinion, were not deserving of praise. Cherry refused to allow him to dampen her spirits; they were all heroes so far as she was concerned, even those who were eliminated the moment they left the chute.

In the end she decided that she liked and admired the clowns best of all. Although their antics made the audience howl with laughter, Torry had told Cherry that their serious job was to distract the attention of the fierce Brahma bulls whenever a contestant was in danger.

They left Tucson around eleven o'clock, and as the twinkling lights of the city slid away behind them, Cherry's exhilaration ebbed away. Tomorrow was going to be an awful day! If only she could count on finding in her mailbox some letters from home. She and Torry had left the ranch that morning while Mr. Conrad was still sorting the mail. Surely the package of dresses would be waiting for her. *And* a stack of letters.

Cherry said good night to Torry on the moonlit patio and tiptoed across the living room and into the office. Her box was empty as usual. "One of the maids probably put it in my room," she decided.

She hurried back across the living room, walking on the rugs in order to be as quiet as possible, and opened the door to her cubbyhole. The moonlight was streaming through the doors and everything was exactly as she had left it. The uniforms which she had hung in various parts of the room to air, looked like headless, legless ghosts in the weird light.

There were deep shadows in the far corners. In one of them there just had to be the package from home. Cherry switched on the light. The shadows fled leaving empty corners. There wasn't even a post card on her bureau or desk or dressing table. Cherry fought back tears of disappointment. Resolutely she put away her uniforms and undressed.

"Grow up," she said to herself sternly. "There are a dozen answers to why you haven't heard from home or from the gang. Everybody's busy, for one thing. And they could have forgotten to put air-mail stamps on the letters. And the package could have got lost or delayed in transit."

She switched off the light and to her surprise found herself in complete darkness. During the past half hour the moon must have traveled to a point where the roof of the hacienda hid it from view. She groped her way over to the double glass doors. One half of the patio was in deep shadow; the other half was almost as light as day.

But someone was moving through the shadowy section. He was moving stealthily, a shadow within a shadow, and then he emerged for a swift moment in the moonlit section before he slipped inside the living room.

It was Harold Bean, Cherry was sure of that, although she hadn't glimpsed his face. But there was no mistaking his long, awkward strides.

Where had he been? And how dared he leave the hacienda on her night off?

CHAPTER XVI

Cherry Recognizes Her Enemy

PROMPTLY AT SEVEN-THIRTY THE NEXT MORNING, Cherry started off to take her patients' T.P.R.'s. She didn't know whether she was supposed to go on duty then or not until after breakfast, but decided to be on the safe side. She was not sure either if Mrs. Blair and Jackie would allow her inside their suites, but they did, greeting her in stony silence.

Jacqueline maintained her silence throughout breakfast, but the other teen-agers were bubbling over with excitement.

"No classes this afternoon," they told Cherry gaily. "The Bean Pole has gone off for the whole day. We're going to have a study period in the classroom this morning, with you in charge, and then we're going to have a picnic ride."

"Out to The Castle," Patty explained. "Señora said we could if you'd go along. We'll cook our lunch on the barbecue pit. Now that we know for sure there isn't anything valuable hidden out there, we may as well have some fun out of it. Will you go with us, Cherry? Will you?"

"Of course," Cherry said. "If Señora approves."

Señora did more than approve. After breakfast she went to the office and sent for Cherry on the intercom. Cherry had anticipated a disagreeable scene but instead Señora was warm and friendly. "Cherry," she began, "a lot of things have been going on here which I don't understand. I realize now that several times I have unjustly blamed you for situations for which you weren't responsible. I'm afraid I didn't give you the benefit of doubt because I jumped to the wrong conclusion about you. I was told by both Jacqueline and Harold Bean that you constantly complained about the time you had to spend supervising the teen-agers. I have since learned that you have never complained about anything. I cannot imagine why you didn't at least complain about the perfume incident. Jacqueline confessed to me yesterday morning that she committed that crime and many others. I don't know what happened to make her want to unburden her soul and confess her sins, but I hoped that she would immediately apologize to you." Señora smiled ruefully. "She isn't quite ready for that step yet.

But I think she will when she gets to know you better. So I was wondering if you would mind spending a little more time with the teen-agers from now on. I hardly dared make this request when I thought you bitterly resented being treated as a governess."

"I'd love to be with the boys and girls more," Cherry cried impulsively. "But, with the exception of Patty, they all seemed to resent me. Do you really want me to supervise their study period this morning and go on the picnic ride?"

"I'd be more than grateful if you would," Señora replied. "Harold Bean has not had a full day off for a long time. So I could hardly refuse his request today. Although," she added more to herself than to Cherry, "in actual hours he owes me time, not the other way 'round. However, with your co-operation, things will work out very well. Torry will, of course, go along on the picnic ride. But I don't like the boys and girls to go too far away unless a nurse is with them. Accidents can happen and you never can tell when an asthmatic may have an attack."

Cherry nodded. "I'll bring along a first-aid kit and a hypodermic syringe. And a dose of whatever has been prescribed for each one in case of a mild attack."

"Fine," Señora said approvingly. "You probably won't need anything, but it's best to be on the safe side."

So they set off around eleven o'clock with bulging

saddlebags. Because it was so warm under the blazing sun they walked their horses a great deal of the time. Patty told the others then how she and Cherry and Torry had searched The Castle and had found the two notes.

"Let's all search one last time," she finished. "We just might find another note."

"A treasure hunt," Davie shouted. "It's a swell idea, Patty. Whoever finds anything at all gets a prize."

Even Jackie, who had been sulkily silent up until then, said enthusiastically, "Maybe there *is* something valuable hidden out there after all. I think those notes from your father were clues."

"So do I," Cherry said.

"We should have brought spades," Johnny said. "Maybe it's buried treasure."

"Gleeps no!" Richie argued. "We'd have to dig up the whole desert. The way sand shifts around, the treasure might have started out at The Castle and ended up back at the corral."

"It's too hot to dig, anyway," Nancy added.

"I tell you what," Torry said. "While I'm cooking the grub, you kids search The Castle. It'll keep you out of my hair and maybe out of mischief, too, although that's too much to ask."

Cherry promptly made up her mind to investigate the desk again. She had been thinking about those four brass thumbtacks. For one thing they were much larger than the average thumbtack. Suppose one of them was a button which released a spring? Maybe there was a secret compartment way in the back of one of the pigeonholes.

They were in the foothills now and all of a sudden Torry, who had been riding ahead of the troop, uttered a shout of surprise:

"Well, I'll be a monkey's uncle!"

Cherry cantered up to his side. There, parked inside the semicircle of bluffs, was Harold Bean's midget car. And the tall, thin tutor himself was lounging beside it, gazing nonchalantly up at the gleaming tower room of The Castle.

"Say, what goes on?" Torry demanded belligerently as he dismounted. "Thought you were in Nogales, hot on the trail of a Mexican legend which was going to make your thesis deathless prose."

Harold Bean shrugged his bony shoulders and said something which was drowned out by the cries of the teen-agers as they rode around the bluffs and caught sight of him.

"Gleeps," Richie groaned. "Don't tell me we're going to have classes out here on the desert!"

"Oh, *no*," Dickie moaned. "It can't be Bean. It's a mirage. Pay no attention to it, boys and girls, and it'll go away."

"I give up," Nancy said as she slid from her saddle with a loud sigh. "The shock is too much. Now I'll *have* to eat."

Jackie and Johnny yelled in unison: "Oh, go away, Harold Bean. Nobody wants you around."

When at last the uproar died down, Patty marched over to the tutor, leading her horse by the reins, and said quietly, "I guess you don't know that you're trespassing, Harold. All of this land inside the bluffs belongs to me. I think I have a right to ask you what you are doing here."

He shrugged again. "I don't think you can exactly call it trespassing, Patty Doake. Your father and my father bought this piece of land together. They built The Castle together, too. Have you any proof that you are the sole heir?"

"No," Patty said coolly. "Nothing but the deed which you can see any time you like if you'll take the trouble to call on my father's lawyer."

"Moreover," he continued, just as though she hadn't spoken, "I think I have a perfect right to inspect what you might call my ancestral home. For sentimental reasons, and governed, you might say, by curiosity, I decided to forego my trip to Mexico today. I felt I owed it to my father's memory to view at long last this edifice which he erected with his own bare hands. I have waited patiently, Patty Doake, for you to invite me to accompany you on one of your many jaunts out here. You have never honored me with such an invitation."

"Oh, all right," Patty interrupted. "I'm sorry. Come on in." She opened the door and marched stiffly inside. He followed her so closely that Cherry couldn't help laughing. He loomed above Patty like a giant daddy longlegs.

Daddy longlegs! The shadow Patty had seen on the patio early yesterday morning, right after someone had sneaked out of her room! Now suddenly Cherry knew who her enemy was. Cold with horror she realized that he was also Patty's enemy.

Of all the people connected with the ranch, Harold Bean was the only one who had a motive for wanting to get rid of her—even before she arrived. For Cherry could see it all now. She was not the only one who felt sure that something valuable was hidden in The Castle. Harold Bean was equally sure. In fact, it was obvious that he felt whatever was hidden there rightfully belonged to him.

Now Cherry could understand why Harold Bean was willing to work at the ranch for such a small salary. In the beginning he must have thought that it would be a simple matter for him to drive out to The Castle along the old wagon road, climb in through a window, and search for the nest egg. Then he had discovered that he couldn't get in without the key. Had he then decided upon another scheme?

The foothills were temptingly close to the land which he still felt was rightfully his, and so many miles from the ranch proper! Using a forged assay, had Harold Bean been trying to sell Mr. Fleming a purely fictitious mine on property which belonged to the Conrads?

At any rate, last fall Mr. Fleming had apparently made a down payment of five thousand dollars on a purchase agreement. Since then, as Mr. Fleming now suspected, Harold Bean had been stalling him along. So Mr. Fleming had come to Tucson and had issued an ultimatum when he said:

"You will meet me right here with your lawyer and the deed and we'll close the deal. Otherwise, the whole thing is off." Earlier in the conversation he had said:

"When I talked to you on the phone yesterday—"

After that telephone conversation, Harold Bean must have known that his time was running out. So he had probably returned to his original scheme; the theft of Patty's nest egg. That night he had stolen her brown envelope, and on the following Monday morning had sneaked into town to have a duplicate made of the key. He had undoubtedly made a copy of the letter—the letter which Cherry felt sure must contain all of the clues.

But although he had searched The Castle every chance he got from then on, he hadn't found the treasure. Then, eavesdropping one evening on the patio outside of her doors, he must have heard her talking to Patty about the letter they had found in the bedpost. So he had searched Patty's room for it—as recently as yesterday morning when she had seen his shadow on the patio.

And now today, since early morning, he had been out here trying to find the nest egg. It must have been a blow to him when he heard their voices and the sound of their horses' hoofs. He had barely time to get out of the house and lock the door before Torry entered the semicircle. Right now, he was back inside again and Jacqueline was saying disdainfully:

"We came out here to have a treasure hunt. If you're going to hang around, Harold Bean, you may as well help Patty try to find her nest egg, too."

"If only I had some proof of my suspicions!" Cherry thought desperately. "He may find the nest egg before anybody else does."

"I should be glad to help," he said to Jackie, and Cherry couldn't help noticing that he glanced out the corner of one eye at the desk. Immediately he threw back his head and stared up at the tower room. "The cupola," he said emphatically, "is of course the place to search." He started up the circular staircase.

"I hate to agree with him," Jacqueline said in a loud whisper, "but he is a brain, so let's go, gang." They trailed up behind him, pushing and shoving one another amidst much giggling and loud laughter.

"Wild horses couldn't make me search the tower room again," Patty said. "I'm going out to the barbecue pit to see if Torry needs any help."

Cherry moved swiftly over to the desk. She pressed one of the thumbtacks tentatively and then she sensed that someone was staring at her. She wheeled. Harold Bean was coming back down the stairs, taking three steps at a time and moving so awkwardly that he looked as though he might pitch forward and fall to the bottom. Before Cherry could gather her wits, he was at her side.

"A fascinating piece of furniture," he said rather breathlessly. "Cholla wood. The whole unit is made of cholla wood. What painstaking work! It requires a special kind of saw, you know, for cactus wood, impregnated with sand as it is, is extraordinarily tough."

"So I understand," Cherry said, thinking: Oh, dear, he's going to hover at my elbow the whole time. I've got to get rid of him. Aloud she said: "Now that the boys and girls are hunting for the treasure, I think you and I ought to help Torry prepare the lunch. Patty's helping him now, but she really should be searching for her nest egg."

"Quite right," he agreed as he followed her outside.

"I am not what one would call a culinary expert, but I am willing to offer my services for what they may be worth."

And then they heard a scream and a thud, followed by more screams. "Help. Help! Miss Ames." It was Jacqueline's voice, high-pitched and hysterical. "Help! Johnny just fell over the railing."

CHAPTER XVII

~~~~~~

An Unexpected Reunion

WITH HER HEART IN HER THROAT, CHERRY RACED BACK inside The Castle. For a moment, the teen-agers, swarming down the stairs, blocked her view. And then she saw the crumpled body. Johnny was lying on the floor with one ankle bent at an angle which told Cherry at once that it was broken; probably a Colles' fracture. Jackie was kneeling beside him, tugging at his arm, sobbing:

"You're all right, Johnny. There's nothing wrong. Get up and show me that you're all right."

"Don't move him," Cherry cried sharply. "Davie! Get Torry at once and bring in two saddle blankets and several pieces of stirrup leather. Richie! Bring me the medical kit I brought out in my saddlebag."

Johnny, who had been momentarily stunned, was

172

now conscious, groaning with pain. Torry came in and knelt beside him, too. "Thank goodness it's not a compound fracture," Cherry whispered. Together, they gently wrapped him in one of the blankets and lifted him onto the bed.

"I can't stand it," Johnny moaned.

"Do something," Jacqueline screamed. "What kind of nurse are you, anyway? Do something to stop his pain." She flung herself on the floor and buried her face in her arms. Patty and Nancy did their best to comfort her, but she paid no attention to them.

"Never mind, Johnny," Cherry said soothingly. "I have some morphine right here in my kit. I'm going to give you a shot. Then Torry and I are going to splint that ankle. We're going to make a cast for it out of this saddle blanket and the leather straps. After that, you will have hardly any pain at all. In fact, you'll be able to ride back to the hacienda."

In a few minutes Johnny stopped moaning. He looked up at Cherry gratefully. "Gosh, you're some nurse. Gee, thanks."

Jacqueline reached out and timidly touched Cherry's hand. "You're—you're wonderful," she murmured. I— I wish I were dead. I've been so mean to you. Stealing your mail and—and—why, I even took out of our mailbox the air-mail letter you wrote the very first night you came. I—" Suddenly she interrupted herself with a loud cry of rage. Moving swiftly out of the circle around Johnny, she darted across the room. "Harold Bean! You haven't done a thing to help since my brother got hurt. You mean, horrid thing. Sitting there at that desk all the time."

He jumped up and whirled around to face her. If he had been caught on the verge of committing murder he couldn't have looked more guilty.

"I— I—" he stammered. "Why, there was nothing I could do. I was just about to offer my car as the best means of transporting the invalid back to the ranch."

"Darn white of you," Torry growled. "We accept. Now, will you be kind enough to help me carry the boy out to the back seat?"

"Why, certainly," the tutor said. "If you had needed my services before this, you had only to ask."

"Oh, be still!" Jackie yelled. "And you be careful when you carry my brother. You big clumsy thing. If you stumble, I'll— I'll—" She bent down to pick up something which Cherry couldn't see, then she followed the two men out, muttering threats to Harold Bean every step of the way.

Cherry stopped long enough to stoop and peer into the pigeonholes of the desk, and there it was, the secret compartment she felt sure might be there. The backboard of one of the pigeonholes was lying flat. Cherry pressed the front two thumbtacks at once, and it sprang back into place. "Well," she reflected as she hurried out to her patient, "whatever was there, Harold Bean has it now."

"I want to ride back with him, too," Jackie was saying. "Please, may I, Cherry? You sit in the seat with him, and I'll sit in front."

Cherry glanced at Torry. "What about the horses?"

"It's all right," he said. "The boys and I can each lead one." He turned to Harold Bean who was folding himself behind the wheel. "Listen, you! Drive slowly and carefully over that bumpy road. We won't be able to keep up with you on account of the gopher holes. But we'll be watching. Consider that your car has been commandeered. Miss Ames is the boss. Do you understand?"

The tutor nodded and put the car into gear. Cherry couldn't see his face during the long, slow ride back, but his silence told her that he was seething with rage. Jackie did most of the talking. When she wasn't asking Johnny how he was, she was berating Harold Bean. And every now and then she made little sporadic confessions to Cherry in a pleading-for-forgiveness tone of voice.

"I have all of your letters I swiped, Cherry. I didn't open them. There's a big stack. They all arrived one day last week. I saw them in your box and I— I just took them. I was sorry right afterward, but it was too late to put them back. I was scared somebody might catch me." A few minutes later she said:

"I swiped Mrs. Blair's bell and put it in the ice bag, and I put the top of her hairpin box on the jam pot. It just fit. I thought it was funny. I put the alarm clock under her bed, too. I took the Do Not Disturb signs off her door and I squirted your clothes with perfume and— I guess that's all, isn't it Johnny?"

"It's enough," he said drowsily. "We should both be put in stocks, broken ankle and all, and left out on the desert to starve to death."

Cherry laughed. "We'll let bygones be bygones. You've been punished enough, Johnny, and so has Jackie because she's your twin. If one twin suffers any pain, the other suffers too. I know, because, you see, I really and truly am a twin. Charlie doesn't look anything like me now, but he's my twin just the same."

"Oh, I hate myself," Jackie moaned. "When I saw his picture on your bureau I just made up my mind that you'd lied. And I thought you were a tattletale, too. But I know you're not. Cherry, it was you who came into my room Sunday night and took away that scorched towel. When I woke up the next morning and saw the mess, I nearly died of fright. Why, the whole hacienda might have burned to the ground. Why didn't you tell Señora on me?" Before Cherry could answer, she rambled on: "That's why I stayed in my room Monday morning. Johnny sneaked out early and buried the lamp shade and the towel. When Señora came in to see why I was having breakfast in bed, she asked me what had happened to my lamp shade. Then I confessed everything, only I didn't tell her I'd fallen asleep with the light on. I just said it had got scorched because I'd wrapped a towel around it so I could read after Lights Out. All she said was that she hoped I'd never do that again. I didn't know then who had taken off the towel and put out the fire. But it was you, Cherry, wasn't it?"

Cherry nodded. "I probably should have tattled that time, but I felt pretty sure you'd learned your lesson the hard way. I guess we all have to learn the hard way." She added softly, "We're almost home, Jackie. Don't you think you ought to telephone your mother and father and tell them about Johnny's accident?"

"No, I don't," Jackie said stormily. "Our mother doesn't care anything about us."

"I think she does," Cherry insisted. "You've never given her a chance to prove it, that's all. Johnny's fracture isn't serious, but if you call her and say that he'd like her to spend some time with him while the bones are knitting, I'm sure she'd come."

"Never given her a chance," Johnny repeated in surprise. "Gosh, I never thought about it that way. What you mean, Cherry, is that if *we* acted as though we wanted a mother, *she* might act more like one?"

It was Jackie who answered the question. "Cherry's right, Johnny," she cried impulsively. "When Mother got to be a star we stopped treating her like a mother. It isn't her fault that we can't all live together the whole year round. If we didn't have asthma we'd be in Beverly Hills right now. I'm going to call her up first chance I get."

Harold Bean parked his car beside the patio, and before anyone could climb out, Señora rushed through the double doors.

"Oh, Cherry," she almost sobbed. "I'm so glad you're back. Mrs. Blair has had a serious attack. The doctor is here and we're giving her helium and oxygen." Then she caught sight of Johnny, wrapped in the saddle blanket, his head on Cherry's lap. "Good heavens. What has happened?"

"A fractured ankle," Cherry said succinctly. "Thank goodness Dr. Monroe is here."

For the next few hours Cherry felt as though she were moving through a nightmare. She and Señora dashed from one patient to the other. And Dr. Monroe seemed to be everywhere at once. An ambulance was sent for. Johnny was taken to the hospital where his ankle was set and put in a cast. Then, mainly because Jackie refused to be separated from him, he was brought back to their suite after he had reacted from the anesthetic. By that time, Mrs. Blair was breathing normally, but could not be left alone. Someone must sit with Johnny all night, too.

"I don't know what to do," Kirk Monroe said to Señora and Cherry. "I can't get hold of even one special, let alone two. And you gals can't take it all night and tomorrow morning, too. I'm not even sure I can get a special then."

They had gone to the office for a hurried consultation. Patty was sitting with Mrs. Blair, and Jackie was with her brother. Suddenly the phone rang. Señora snatched it up. "Miss Ames? Just a minute, please."

Cherry was so tired she didn't even wonder who might be calling her. "Hello," she said listlessly.

"Ames! What's the matter with you?" It was Gwen Jones. Cherry could hardly believe her ears.

"Didn't you get our letter?"

"No," Cherry said weakly.

"Well, that's funny," Gwen said. "Josie and I are at the Westerner. We decided to take your advice and spend our vacation out here. We kept wondering why you didn't call us, so we finally decided to call you."

"Gwen," Cherry gasped, "if we send a handsome young foreman for you, can you come out at once? Both of you."

"Natch," Gwen said with a chuckle. "But are we invited?"

"Are you ever," Cherry said, and explained. "It's awful to ask you to go on duty while you're on vacation, but—"

"Think nothing of it," Gwen said cheerfully. "You know Josie and me. We're never really happy out of uniform. And working at the same hacienda with you will be a treat."

"Thanks," Cherry breathed and put the phone back in its cradle. "Two registered nurses," she told Kirk and Señora, "will be out here just as soon as Torry can bring them."

"You're a wonder," Kirk and Señora said in one voice. "Well," Kirk added, "I guess you've got everything under control. So I'll run along. You know where to call me if you should need me."

Two hours later Gwen and Josie arrived. Cherry gave them a brief hug and kiss apiece, introduced them to Señora and their patients, and then she and Señora went to the dining room for dinner. Neither one of them had had a bite to eat since breakfast and they were weak from hunger and exhaustion.

After they gave the waitress their order, Señora said, "Cherry, Mrs. Blair's attack was brought on by the fact that I told her Jackie had confessed to all of the pranks for which she had blamed you. She flatly refused to believe me, and I foolishly argued with her. Then when she was finally convinced she felt so ashamed of herself that she burst into tears. I did everything possible to calm her down, but you know Mrs. Blair."

"Oh, dear," Cherry said, "I *am* a Calamity Jane."

"Not you," Señora said with a chuckle. "You're a magician. Producing two nurses out of your hat like that!" She bent forward and lowered her voice: "Another thing. Harold Bean has resigned."

"Resigned?" Cherry was so surprised she jumped.

Señora nodded. "Frank gave him a good talking to a while ago. He laid down the law. He said that from now on Harold would have a day off once a week, just as you do. And at other times he would have to stay here. Harold didn't like that at all. He quit. Went to his room, packed, and drove off for Tucson in a swirl of gravel." Señora sighed. "He *was* a good tutor, but Mr. Neap has recommended his nephew who I feel sure will be even better."

The teen-agers were coming in from the patio now. Cherry waved and smiled. For this one meal they would have to eat without the supervision of an adult and she knew that they were still so shocked by Johnny's accident that they would behave. Then she noticed that Jackie, still on the terrace, was beckoning to her.

Cherry hurried to join her, thinking that Johnny must have asked for her.

Jackie slipped her arm through Cherry's and giving it a hug said, "You were right about Mother. She's flying to Tucson on the first plane she can get. Father is coming too! And Mother's going to stay until they take off Johnny's cast." She drew Cherry off to one corner of the terrace and handed her a slip of crumpled paper. "I thought you might like to read this when you read your mail. It's all in your top bureau drawer, Cherry. But this note I found out at The Castle. Harold Bean dropped it when he jumped up suddenly from the desk. He didn't see me when I picked it up. I started to read it and then I realized it must have been written by Patty's father. I showed it to her and she told me to give it to you."

There was just enough light from the rising moon so Cherry could read the spidery scrawl. Patty joined them then.

"It's only another one of those little pearls of wisdom," Patty said discouragedly. "I give up."

"I'm not so sure of that," Cherry said, tucking the note into her uniform pocket. "I have a feeling that there's an important clue in Note No. 3."

CHAPTER XVIII

Cherry Makes Up Her Mind

IT HAD BEEN A LONG, EXCITING DAY BUT AT LAST THE
house was quiet. Cherry took off her rumpled uniform,
showered, and donned a pair of warm pajamas. She
climbed into bed sure that she would fall asleep from
sheer exhaustion the minute her head hit the pillow.

But although her body was tired her mind refused to
rest. All afternoon and evening, frantically busy with
the two emergency cases, she had had to push the mystery way down into her subconscious mind. Now it was
uppermost, and her thoughts made her eyelids stay
propped wide open. Finally, in desperation, Cherry
turned on the night-table light and got out of bed.

From the toe of her riding boot she took the brown
envelope in which were all of the letters Mr. Doake had

183

written to Patty. Cherry got back into bed and read
them again carefully. Why had he said he was a champion pole vaulter when he hadn't even gone to college?
Was there some connection between that phrase and
"my vaulting ambition" in the letter which the lawyer
had found under the old man's pillow with the key to
The Castle? And what was the clue, if any, in the note
which Jacqueline had picked up out at The Castle that
morning after Harold Bean dropped it?

> *"My darling daughter:*
> *"Remember that the immortal Shakespeare*
> *wrote: 'He who steals my purse steals trash.'*
> *What you are seeking is so lowly that it is be-*
> *neath your notice."*

Cherry thoughtfully ran her hands through her dark
curls. Harold Bean had had plenty of time in which to
read that note; in fact, he probably knew it by heart.
The tutor was no fool. If there was a clue hidden between the lines he must have discovered it long ago. But
the fact that he had resigned seemed to indicate that he,
like Patty, had given up.

Then suddenly it dawned on Cherry that Harold
Bean had resigned so that he could continue to search
The Castle day and night from now on if necessary. He
was afraid to wait until his next day off, for fear Cherry
and Patty might find the treasure first.

Cherry began to tingle with excitement. He had been headed for Tucson when he drove off in a swirl of gravel, but he could easily have left the driveway before he reached the main road and driven straight across the desert to The Castle. Now that midget car of his made sense. About a mile east of the bunkhouse there was a ridge of low bluffs that ran between the driveway and the old wagon road. The top of a larger car cutting across the desert in the daytime would have been seen by one of the cowboys, but the midget roadster was just the right height.

This fact explained Harold Bean's unexpected appearance at The Castle this morning. He was probably there now.

No, that didn't make sense, Cherry decided, after thinking it over. There was no reason for him to handicap himself by searching at night when he would have to use a flashlight and probably a kerosene lantern as well. Tomorrow morning would be soon enough. He would drive out from Tucson at dawn, and he could camp out at The Castle with nothing to fear from Cherry and Patty until next Sunday. So far as Harold Bean knew, Cherry could not leave her two patients until her next day off—if then. He had no way of knowing that two registered nurses had arrived shortly after his angry departure. He had heard Kirk Monroe say that there was an acute shortage of R.N.'s in Tucson;

and he had no way of knowing that Gwen and Josie were there on vacation but willing to help out.

Cherry chuckled. "As Mr. Doake would say, 'A friend in need is a friend indeed.' Two friends are even better!"

Thinking of Patty's father made Cherry turn back to the note which she was sure Harold Bean had found in the secret compartment of the desk's recess. And then the phrase, "beneath your notice" seemed to stand out from the page as though the words had been written in red ink.

Beneath your notice must mean under the alcove, where the note had been hidden. Although the desk, like the rest of the unit, looked as though it had been built-in, there was a good chance that it only *looked* that way. Maybe you could pull it away from the wall. And maybe underneath it was a trap door! Now the *vault* in *vaulting* and *vaulter* made sense.

Cherry scrambled out of bed and began to dress quickly. There *had* to be a trap door under the alcove, and beneath the door was a vault in which Mr. Doake had hidden Patty's nest egg. Automatically, without realizing what she was doing, she put on a fresh uniform, and because it was very cold outdoors at this time of night, she slipped on her warm jacket.

The trap door must be found before morning when she was sure Harold Bean would arrive at The Castle.

She herself couldn't drive out there to look for it, but Torry could. And he would, because he was just as interested in finding Patty's nest egg as she was.

Someone tapped on Cherry's door, and Gwen came into the room, quietly closing the door behind her.

In a loud whisper she demanded: "What in the world are you doing in uniform at this time of night, Cherry Ames? You're off duty until tomorrow morning. Orders from both the Conrads, and seconded by me and Josie."

Cherry suppressed a giggle. "I didn't realize I was in whites. I'm so excited I don't know what I'm doing. Don't ask me a lot of questions now, Gwen, but I think I'm on the verge of solving that mystery I sort of hinted at earlier this evening."

Gwen groaned. "Why must you always solve your mysteries all by your lonesome? Have you forgotten that just last summer, when you were working at the Hilton Clinic, you tried to capture a bunch of crooks single-handed and almost ended up in the bottom of the stand-pipe in that old mill? Do I have to remind you of the fact that when you were a night supervisor—"

"*Sh-h*," Cherry interrupted. "I'm not going to do anything about this mystery myself. I'm simply going out to the bunkhouse and ask Torry to solve it for me."

Gwen rolled her eyes. "That handsome, handsome cowboy! And how he dotes on you. Well, I guess you're safe in his hands. I only dropped in because I saw your light shining under the door and thought maybe you'd fallen asleep and forgotten to turn it off." She smugly patted her perky cap into place. "I'm getting to be quite a detective myself. Indoors and in the patio, what with all those double glass doors and gigantic picture windows amounts to the same thing as being outdoors, it's as light as day. But the moon is riding high in the sky now and it casts a shadow along this wall of the patio. Not everybody, I'll have you know, would have noticed the crack of light under your door. But to me it stood out like a sore thumb."

"You're wonderful," Cherry cried impatiently. "Now please bring that ice bag with—I hope, ice in it—back to Mrs. Blair and let me go on about my business."

They slipped quietly out into the moonlit patio and soundlessly formed with their lips, "Good-by and good luck" to each other. Cherry flew along the path to the bunkhouse. All of the lights were out but Torry's cubicle was so close to the door she was sure he would hear when she knocked and called his name as loudly as she dared.

"Torry. Torry. It's Cherry."

At last the door opened but the cowboy who stood at the entrance sleepily rubbing his eyes wasn't Torry. It was Bill. He was clutching with one hand a flamboyant Indian blanket that trailed over one of his broad shoulders, and he mumbled:

"Whatsha matter? You want Torry, Miss Cherry? He ain't here."

"Oh, Bill," Cherry wailed. "Where is he? When will he be back?"

"Dunno," Bill said, slowly waking up. "I know *where* he is. In Tucson. He went in to buy a saddle some rich dude wants to sell dirt cheap. But when he'll be back, I can't tell you, ma'am. Torry, he likes to bargain. Might take him all night to get that dude to come down to his price."

"Well, all right," Cherry said, trying to disguise her disappointment. "Thanks and good night, Bill. I'm sorry I disturbed you."

"No trouble at all. Don't mention it." The young cowboy closed the door as Cherry turned away.

And then she saw that Torry's jalopy was parked beside the corral. So he must have gone to town in the ranch's station wagon. Suddenly Cherry made up her mind. Torry, she knew, always left his keys in the ignition lock. It was too much of a temptation. Almost before she knew it she was behind the wheel, starting the motor.

The ancient Model A Ford bucked like a bronco a few times and then, under her capable hands, settled down to bumping slowly over the ruts in the old wagon road that led out to The Castle.

CHAPTER XIX

Hidden Treasure

~~~~~~

TO CHERRY IT SEEMED AS THOUGH IT WERE EVEN lighter than day out on the desert. The weird, gilt-painted tower room gleamed with startling brightness, and since the rest of The Castle was hidden by the bluffs which semicircled it, the cupola looked as though it were suspended in mid-air.

Cherry shivered as much from cold as from nervousness. "That tower room looks like a golden finger of warning, pointing to the sky," she said to herself, deliberately talking out loud to keep her courage up. "I'm glad I had sense enough to put the key and all the clues into my jacket pocket while Gwen was asking me all those questions. Good old Gwen! How she would love to be with me, now, to help me find the treasure. But that couldn't be! If she and Josie were not on duty I couldn't have left."

The cacti and clumps of mesquite that lined the road stood in pools of blue-black shadows that matched the larger pools cast by the midnight-blue bluffs.

In the bright sunlight of the daytime the vast expanse of the desert had not seemed frightening at all. The brilliant colors of the sunlit panorama had been so gorgeous that even if she had visited The Castle alone heretofore she would not have felt frightened. It was all so fabulously unreal that you felt as though you were living through one of the nicest kind of dreams.

But now in the moonlight, the desert was a terribly isolated and lonely place, and the dream became sort of a nightmare. Cherry parked the car beside The Castle and sat there for a minute, steeling herself. As she massaged the numbness from her cold fingers she told herself firmly that she would have to go inside and try to move the strange desk. She knew that if the backboard of it was not—as she hoped it wasn't—the wall behind it, it would be easy to move.

"Empty and unattached," Cherry said to herself in a whisper, "it's probably as light as a piece of cork. I can't imagine why Patty and I—*and* Harold Bean— never thought of trying to move it."

Talking to herself still, Cherry took from the door pocket the big flashlight Torry always kept there, climbed out of the car, and forced her shaking legs to carry her to the door of The Castle. It was all so eerie and quiet and remote that she couldn't help jumping at the click the key made when she turned it in the lock. Once inside the big, triangular-shaped ground-floor room, she instinctively played her torch along the circular staircase and the balcony above it.

Then she hurried to the big patch of light which streamed through the skylight in the tower room. Although the panes of glass in the ceiling window were dusty, the moon seemed to Cherry to be a giant flashlight shining, for her special purposes, right on the desk. She switched off Torry's torch for fear the batteries might be old, laid it on the floor, and grabbed one corner of the desk with both hands.

To her surprise and delight it came out from the wall with the greatest of ease. Another yank, and there it was, thickly coated with dust—a heavy ring which must be the handle of a trap door of steel! Ignoring the dust, and again using both hands, Cherry tugged at the ring. As she pulled it toward her, a small section of the floor made of steel, which had been concealed by the desk, came up with the ring.

Through the narrow opening Cherry could see that a three-stepped ladder led down to a vault below. Her hands and feet were icy cold as she grabbed the flashlight and climbed down into it. Once there, in the small steel-walled room, Cherry felt as though she were in a steel vault, except, thank goodness, the steel door was raised.

"I never thought I'd suffer from claustrophobia," she reflected with a nervous chuckle, "but I certainly am now."

The section of the wall which was lighted by the moon was as smooth as glass, but the opposite wall, which was in shadow, she soon found out contained an opening. In a second she saw that the opening was really nothing but a built-in strongbox, and the door was ajar. She simply swung it open and played the beam of her flashlight inside. Then she uttered a gasp of amazement and disappointment. Resting on a long white envelope was an ugly chunk of rock.

Cherry felt like crying. How could Mr. Doake have been so eccentric? To build such an expensive vault for the sole purpose of hiding a worthless piece of stone! Listlessly she rolled the rock way back into the box and took out the envelope. It was unsealed and addressed in Mr. Doake's handwriting:

To Whom It May Concern

Cherry climbed back up the ladder and perched on the top step. She hesitated for a moment and then drew out the folded sheets of paper the envelope contained. On the first page the words To Whom It May Concern were repeated, but they were followed by:

"I hope the finder of this letter is my precious daughter, Patricia. But if not, you, the finder, must read this letter and deliver it to her as soon as you can. The stone which was resting on this letter is an uncut emerald worth about fifty thousand dollars . . ."

Cherry gasped, this time from joy and amazement. So that's what the ugly chunk of rock was! Thank goodness Harold Bean hadn't got here first.

"You, the reader," the letter continued, "may or may not know that I spent most of my adult life speculating. It all began on my eighteenth birthday forty years ago when I inherited five thousand dollars from my grandfather. My best friend, Thomas Bean, persuaded me to invest it in land five miles from the center of Tucson. Tom was a born speculator and he was sure that there was gold on this land. But there wasn't a grain of it, so I, a penniless orphan, had to go back to work in the laundry where I was earning only a dollar a day. Then suddenly the real-estate boom started. Almost overnight guest ranches began to appear everywhere as tourists and asthma sufferers began to pour into Tucson. I was offered ten thousand dollars for my piece of land, but Tom persuaded me to wait. In the end I sold it for forty thousand dollars—a fortune to a boy of nineteen! Tom and I decided to pool our resources—and that was the beginning.

"The gambling fever was in my veins. We speculated

in everything from real estate to stocks and bonds. We traveled all over the country, sometimes so rich that we rode in special trains—at other times so poor that we had to ride the rods.

"After my marriage I settled down in Tucson for a while, but when Patty's mother died, I again joined forces with Tom. I left my baby daughter with my dear friends, the Conrads, and Tom and I flew to Alaska. After that, I only saw Patty in between speculations and when I was flush with money. I always left plenty of funds with the Conrads for her care and education before starting off again. When I was down on my luck I did not communicate with her.

"But I was constantly nagged by the fear that the time might come when I could not recoup my losses. So I decided to provide Patty with a nest egg. What could it be? The dollar, I had learned from sad experience, could fluctuate from a hundred cents to a quarter with amazing rapidity. Stocks and bonds were even more unreliable in my opinion. A precious jewel—that was the thing!

"Tom and I bought an emerald mine in South America. We worked it ourselves and at last it yielded the stone you have seen. I immediately offered to buy Tom's share of it, but he refused for he had been thinking along the same lines that I had. He wanted to preserve the emerald as a nest egg for his son, Harold. All the way back to Tucson we argued and finally reached a compromise. It began, as usual, with a bet.

" 'I'll bet you don't stay settled down in Tucson,' Tom said to me.

" 'I'll bet I do,' said I.

" 'If you stay put longer than I do,' said he, 'I'll sell you my share of the stone.'

" 'Fair enough,' said I. 'Shake.'

"So we bought from the Conrads an acre of land out on the desert, dug a hole, built a steel vault for the emerald, and erected an odd-shaped house above it. The pie shape of the ground floor amused us for we each owned a slice of the emerald. Before the house was furnished, the fever began to burn in Tom. Whenever it burned in me I would climb up into the tower room and gaze out over the vast desert and satisfy my wanderlust by reliving my past.

"But Tom would only brood as he worked with the cactus wood. Then one day he came to me and said:

" 'You win. Uranium is the thing nowadays. I'm going out after it. Give me my share of the stone in cash, and when I come back from Alaska, I'll be rich enough to play marbles with emeralds that size.'

"He left with the cash and a year later died penniless. I immediately had my lawyer send his son a check for ten times the assessed valuation of The Castle and the land around it. I wish I could do more for Harold but, except for a few hundred dollars I have cached in the hollow post of the sofa bed, all of my funds are tied up. The income from those investments goes to the Conrads for Patty. Some day, even without the emerald, she may be a very rich young lady."

Cherry sighed. She knew what had happened to those investments. When Mr. Doake died he had been virtually down to his last dollar—the money she had found inside the bed post with the first note. If he had known that he had again gambled on Wall Street and lost, he would surely have told Patty about the emerald. The letter had been written three years ago. At that time he had not dared to share the secret with her. Knowledge of the hiding place of such a precious stone was too dangerous.

"I almost wish *I* didn't know about it," Cherry reflected. "I wish I could leave it where it is and put everything back in place until Mr. Conrad can come out and cope with the emerald. But I don't dare. Harold Bean read the note with the important clue in it. He must have figured out that *beneath your notice*, combined with the clues in the first letter, meant that there was a vault under the desk."

"I certainly did!"

Cherry was so startled that she almost fell off the ladder. She had been thinking out loud, but she couldn't have imagined hearing those words which had been uttered in Harold Bean's high, nasal voice.

Slowly she twisted her head around to face the door. There he was on the threshold, and in the moonlight he looked more than ever like Ichabod Crane. He had a gun in one hand and with the other he was pushing his horn-rimmed spectacles back on his nose. Cherry had been frightened at the sight of the gun, but the habitual nervous gesture made her laugh.

"My goodness," she said airily. "How you startled me! I guess the sound of my own voice drowned out your footsteps. But I can't imagine why I didn't hear your car's motor. Did you come out on a flying carpet?"

"Don't be funny." With his long, ungainly strides he hurried over to her and snatched the letter from her hand.

Rather than have it torn, Cherry let him take it. He was wearing a heavy turtleneck sweater instead of the patch-sleeved tweed jacket he usually wore on cold mornings, and he crammed the letter into the hip pocket of his shiny blue serge pants.

"You have no business crumpling that letter like that," Cherry said tartly. "It belongs to Patty. You know what a spidery scrawl Mr. Doake's penmanship was. Mussing the paper isn't going to make it any easier to read."

An evil smile flickered across his pasty face. "I don't have to read it. I just don't want to leave anything lying around. As soon as you hand over that rock I'm going to gag you and tie you up and leave you down in that vault you so cleverly found. Then I'll close the trap door, put the desk back in place and," he finished with a leer, "that will take care of you."

Terror swept over Cherry. It was true, there was nothing she could do to keep him from carrying out his threat. No one knew where she was, and even if they searched The Castle for her, they would never find her —not until it was too late, anyway.

"Hand over that rock!"

Cherry swallowed the lump of fear that was rising in her throat. "What rock?" she forced herself to ask him coldly.

"Listen, Ames." He reached down and touched the tip of her nose with the barrel of his gun. "My father left me some clues, too, see? He told me when he came back from South America that he had brought a nest egg for me with him. I knew it must be hidden in The Castle because he and Mr. Doake spent most of their time working out here until they moved in for good. They didn't build this crazy old place for fun. The very fact that they wouldn't allow a workman—or anyone else for that matter—near the site made me sure that they planned to hide something valuable in The Castle."

As Cherry listened, her fright began to ebb slowly away. If he were not such a despicable character she could have felt sorry for Harold Bean. He might have developed into another kind of man if his father had kept his promise.

"Furthermore," Harold Bean continued in that ponderous way of his, "my father dropped some hints in answer to my curious questions. Once he said that a clue lay in the *Arabian Nights*. Later, on separate occasions, he specified Sinbad the Sailor and Aladdin. Remember the giant roc in *Sinbad*? It didn't take me long to figure out that clue since Father and Mr. Doake had just come back from a mining expedition in South America. The Aladdin clue I didn't figure out until yesterday when I found a note hidden in a secret compartment of the desk. Then I recalled that Aladdin's uncle had sent him down into an underground cavern to fetch the wonderful lamp. So don't sit there and ask me foolish questions like 'What rock?'"

"All right," Cherry said, "I won't." She started to get up, but he pushed her back so roughly that she almost toppled down into the vault. Anger swept away the last bit of fear as she said, "I haven't got the rock, and anyway, it doesn't belong to you. If you'll read that letter you'll discover that your father sold his share of it to Patty's father. The emerald belongs to Patty."

"*Emerald?*" His pale eyebrows shot up. "I didn't dare hope for such a precious stone. I thought it might be a large piece of gold ore. I didn't dare hope for a precious stone. Where is it?" He was so excited that he absent-mindedly placed the pistol on the desk and stooped to grab her shoulders with both hands. "I'll shake you until your teeth fall out if you don't hand it over at once."

Cherry winced with pain, but she knew now that she could outwit him if she kept her head. The story of Aladdin had given her the idea. Knowing how greedy the tutor was she had deliberately told him that the rock was an emerald. And she had been right. The very word had made him lose his head.

"It's down in the vault," she told him. "If you'll just let me stand up and get out of your way, you can go down and get it yourself."

He yanked her to her feet and pushed her away from the narrow entrance. Ignoring the steps of the little ladder, he swung down. As he bent to peer into the open strongbox, Cherry grabbed the gun. At the same moment she heard in the distance the roar of a car's motor. Someone, who was driving faster than it was safe, was coming.

Harold Bean heard the sound, too, and immediately straightened. He was so tall that the whole upper part of his body loomed above the floor. When he saw the gun Cherry was pointing at him, his loose-lipped mouth fell open with surprise.

In the habitual nervous gesture, his hand went to his glasses. "You—you—I—I," he stuttered.

"That's right," Cherry said. "If you'd been as smart

as Aladdin's uncle you would have made me go down after the emerald." Thank goodness he had no way of knowing that she had never shot off a gun in her life, and that even if she had known how to shoot, she wouldn't have pulled the trigger for anything in the world. From the roar, the car must now be only a few yards away. The thing to do was to keep Harold Bean standing there with that look of utter amazement on his face until help came.

"You're smart in some ways, Harold Bean," Cherry chattered on, hoping that he wouldn't notice how her hand that was holding the gun was shaking. "But you're awfully stupid in others."

He started to say something, but the driver of the approaching car had cut the motor, and a man's deep voice was calling:

"Cherry! Cherry! Are you all right?"

It was Torry, and in another minute he was striding inside The Castle. Cherry didn't dare turn around to look at him, but she heard him shout with surprise:

"Hey! What goes on?"

Cherry was too weak with relief to say a word. When he was close enough, she gratefully handed him the gun.

"Take over, Torry, please," she finally got out.

"Delighted, I'm sure," he said in a sarcastic imitation of the tutor. "Although the pleasure won't be mine for long. Up from the depths, you cheap crook," he added to Harold Bean. "A police detective and Mr. Fleming are waiting for you at the hacienda. You may be interested in knowing that the Conrads were not exactly pleased to discover that you've been trying to sell a nonexistent tungsten mine on property which belongs to them!"

CHAPTER XX

"Hasta la Vista"

"WHAT I DON'T UNDERSTAND," PATTY ASKED BEWILDER-edly, "is how Mr. Fleming happened to arrive at the airport on the same plane with the twins' parents."

"That was just a coincidence," Cherry said.

It was almost noon and they had gathered together on the sunlit patio—Gwen and Cherry and Patty and Torry, who had just come back from town with the mail. None of them, except Patty, had slept a wink the night before.

"Mr. and Mrs. Longman," Cherry continued, "got on that plane because of last-minute cancellations, but Mr. Fleming, as Harold Bean knew, had reserved a seat on Monday. He was supposed to meet Mr. Fleming in the waiting room, but of course he had no intention of keeping the appointment. He planned to be in another state by then, *with* your nest egg, Patty."

"I know," Patty said. "And if it hadn't been for you, Cherry—"

"Don't interrupt," Cherry interrupted with a grin. "Mr. Fleming didn't wait long because he was pretty sure that he had been duped. He went to the police and showed them the photographs and maps Harold Bean had sent him. They recognized the property as the foothills near The Castle, pictures of which had appeared in the papers when Mr. Doake died. So one of the detectives drove Mr. Fleming out here to talk over the matter with the Conrads."

"They arrived," Torry added, "at about the same time that I got back from Tucson and a short while after Mrs. Longman arrived in a cab. All the lights in the Conrads' suite were blazing, so naturally I went inside to find out what was cookin'."

"That's what *I* don't understand," Cherry complained. "You must have thought that I was sound asleep in my room, so how did you happen to arrive at The Castle in the nick of time, Torry?"

"Wal now, ma'am," Torry drawled, "it was like this, ma'am. When I parked the station wagon by the patio I saw right off that my jalopy was missin'. While Mrs. Longman, the Conrads, the pow-leeceman, and Mr. Fleming were all shootin' the breeze at once, I slipped out. I woke up everybody in the bunkhouse trying to find out which one of them ornery critters had made off with my gasoline bronco. Then Bill, he woke up enough to tell me that you'd been asking for me, ma'am, and that he'd seen you drive off in my jalopy toward the old wagon road. Now, ma'am, what did you expect me to do? Sit on my hands until you came back?"

"Leave out the *ma'ams*, puh-leeze," Cherry said with a laugh. "So you followed me out to The Castle to accuse me of car-stealing?"

He shook his head gravely. "Seriously, Cherry, I was frantic when I realized that you'd gone out there alone. The car could have broken down or run out of gas. What on earth made you act so foolish, Calamity?"

"I just didn't stop to think about what might have happened," Cherry admitted. "I was plenty scared when I arrived, but I would have been a lot more scared if I'd known that Harold Bean had arrived first. He'd just parked his car in the foothills about half a mile from The Castle when he heard a car coming along the old wagon road. He didn't know who was driving the car, of course, until he sneaked down from the hills. When he saw your jalopy parked by the entrance, Torry, he naturally expected to find you inside. Hence the gun. It must have been a happy moment for him when he peered through the crack in the door and saw poor defenseless me."

"But what an awful moment for you," Gwen said with a shudder. "Honestly, Cherry, I don't know why you didn't faint with fright when he threatened to shut you up in that secret vault."

"I can't bear to think about that," Patty said, shivering. "If anything had happened to you, Cherry, it would have been all my fault."

"Let's talk about something pleasant," Cherry suggested. "The twins for instance. Did you know, Patty, that as soon as Johnny can walk they're going home with their mother? Dr. Monroe thinks that their reconciliation with her may work such wonders that neither of them will ever have a serious attack of asthma again." She gave Patty a quick hug. "And as for you, why you've as good as won your cap already! But what makes me happiest is that you've finally agreed to let the Conrads adopt you."

"I'm happy about that, too," Patty said. "I—"

"You were a silly gal," Torry interrupted sternly, "not to have let your lawyer arrange that long ago. They don't love you because you're rich. They love you because they've always felt that you were their daughter."

"I know," Patty admitted shamefacedly. "But just the same it's nice to know that my own father will be paying my expenses until I'm graduated from nursing school. After that, I have a full-time job waiting for me. Mrs. Blair wants me to be her special for as long as she lives.

That is, of course," she added hastily, "if I'm lucky enough to win my cap."

"You'll win it all right," Cherry said. "You're a grand little nurse already, Patty. I don't know what we would have done without you yesterday."

Just then, Josie appeared, waving a letter. "For you, Cherry. From home. I just happened to be passing the office and Mr. Conrad asked me to bring it right out to you."

Cherry ripped open the envelope. "It's from Mother," she said. "Does anyone object if I read it now?"

"Go right ahead," they all chorused.

Torry added in an ominous aside: "I still think Jackie ought to be spanked for hiding Cherry's mail."

"Oh, oh!" Cherry cried excitedly. "Gwen! Josie! That convalescent home which I told you just opened in Hilton wants me to be the resident nurse as soon as I leave here in May."

"Wonderful." Gwen's green eyes sparkled. "It's only a stone's throw from your home, isn't it, Cherry?"

"Less than an hour's drive," Cherry told her.

"Lucky gal," Josie said enviously. "I've always wanted to work in a rest home. You meet all kinds of people in all stages of recovery from all kinds of illnesses."

"That's right," Gwen heartily agreed. "A convalescent home has all the good points of a hospital, but it's more interesting because the cases are so varied. Instead of just taking care of post-ops, for instance, you get new mothers with their babies, too. Lots of people can't go straight home from a hospital. They're not really sick, but neither are they well enough to take up their lives again without more rest and nursing care."

Cherry chuckled. "Well, I'm glad you two like the idea so much. Because there are jobs waiting for you in Hilton, too. Mother says I'm to chose my own assistants. I'll need a night nurse and a day nurse. You and Josie are the answer, Gwen. When one is on duty, the other can sleep in my room at home. What do you think?"

"It's super-glamorous perfect." Gwen hugged Cherry. "I accept as of now."

Josie ecstatically hugged them both. "We're like the Three Musketeers. No matter where our jobs take us, we always seem to end up all together again."

"Oh, I wish I were an R.N. right now," Patty said wistfully to Torry.

"So do I," he replied mournfully. "How do you suppose I'm going to feel when the desert is in full bloom and I'll have to say to Cherry *'Hasta la vista'*?"

Gwen cupped one hand around her ear. "Come again," she said to Torry. "No spik Spanish."

"Hasta la vista," Cherry explained, "is a lovely way of saying good-bye. Literally it means until the next visit."

"In my language," Torry said, "it means 'Be seein

you.' I'm not going to wait for your next visit to Arizona, Cherry Ames. I'm going to follow you to your home town next summer."

"Grand," Cherry said. "Be sure to bring Patty with you. We'll have a house party." She stared dreamily out across the desert. It was hard to believe that only a few days ago she had been so miserable. She knew now that when she did leave Arizona she would regretfully say *"Hasta la vista,"* and hope that her next visit to this wonderful state would be soon.